Introduction

When setting out to write my first book, 'Guardian Angel,' I had no sense that I would go on and complete a sequel to this story. And yet here it is now!

My initial aim in writing 'Guardian Angel' was to communicate some of the philosophies through which my business, Change Management International, worked, as well as some of the techniques we employed. However, it became a bit more than this I believe, with an under-lying thread relating to the accepted consensus reality of how organisations are run and the ways in which success is measured and attained.

On returning from my first visit to Peru in 2003, I agreed with myself that the story should be carried forward… especially as so many people had asked me "what happened next?"

It may appear to some readers that the book has been written in response to the collapse in the banking system and the economy, with the ensuing dismay at the greed and arrogance displayed by many of the protagonists. In fact, I finished the book in 2006/2007, well before any of the current challenges had kicked off. I hope, however, that some of the insights provide food for thought for the future.

Although change is currently being demanded in the way we run our business and indeed our society, there is the suspicion that people are lying low until the current problems pass, and will then hope to take up where they left off before the crash appeared.

The ensuing story aims to highlight a number of the inappropriate approaches and practices that currently exist in our businesses, many of which appear to have become accepted almost as universal truths. And, in turn, aims to provide direction towards a genuinely new understanding of how organisations can become more engaging and inspiring places in which to work, whilst still producing the financial results necessary to grow and develop. My grateful thanks to all who have assisted me in producing this book – from the mountain shamans of Peru, to my colleague Lucille Hall who has had the task of converting my hand written pages into the readable text which ensues. Thank you all!

And enjoy!

Charlie Jackson
July 2009

"Only when we engage the imagination do we touch people's deepest hopes and fears... and the most powerful means involves the basic and ancient art of story telling"

Tom Morris

Chapter One

New Frontiers

"No one is really stuck in life. We just need wise advisers to show us the way forward."

Tom Morris

A droplet of sweat fell silently onto a leaf beside Douglas's foot. The cacophony of jungle sounds filled his head as he sat on a log wondering what in hell's name had possessed him to take the stuff. Every pore in his body seemed to be leaking the foul substance – each time a little rivulet of sweat found its way to his lips he had to suffer the rancid taste once again.

Douglas was exhausted, having thrown up for over an hour, consumed by the effects of the ayahuasca he had taken around three hours ago.

He was wrestling with the present moment anguish he was experiencing against the potential transformational power of the vision vine of Amazonia. He knew he wouldn't really know of any benefits he was deriving from the experience until he was back into his normal day-to-day life again. Douglas smiled as a beautiful butterfly fluttered across from one ear to the next.

"What is it trying to tell me?" he wondered. "Perhaps it has a transformational message for me?" "Is Lise behind this?"

As he began to smile to himself, another wave of nausea swept over him starting in the pit of his belly and spreading from his stomach through his chest and upwards releasing even more of the disgusting liquid. In his more coherent moments, his mind raced back and forward in amazement at the events of the past two years or so since Lise stepped into his office and his life at 'Guardian Angel.'

Douglas Murray was then CEO of 'Guardian Angel' a moderately sized and successful financial services business. He had been frustrated by what he saw as a basic lack of interest from his people in really improving the performance of the business. Until, that is, he met Lise, a mysterious and magical woman who was working in his Marketing Department. Lise had taken him on a truly magical journey of transformation, which had opened his eyes, in particular, to his part in the perceived lack of success. He had also seen how antiquated ways of thinking about and managing organisations inhibited creativity and the potential of both the people involved and the business itself.

* * *

Douglas could never be quite sure about his experiences with Lise. Being able to become invisible so that he could see what was actually going on in meetings, stepping out of his office on to a plane, or into a football team's dressing room. These weren't just everyday experiences, and not ones he had ever shared with anyone except his wife Pat. Were they real experiences or were they illusions? They had certainly felt real – he remembers feeling real authentic fear when finding himself in a carriage being pulled by six thoroughbred horses and driven by a madman, the latter turning out to be his ego!

The experiences had definitely awakened him, firstly to his self, and to the unproductive and destructive nature of the behaviour that was going on around him in his business, and in the world at large.

He laughed to himself again as he thought of what former colleagues in the financial services world would think of his past and present experiences in his quest for real knowledge. Their world seemed pretty remote to him now. Douglas remembered the mental anguish (as opposed to the physical anguish he was currently experiencing) of the take-over process at Guardian Angel. He had moved from a position of certainty that that was the only way to go, to realising that this may not be the case. He began to waken to the realisation that this belief, that bigger and bigger is better, was not an absolute truth, and was one of many examples of mass hypnosis or conditioning that pervades our world. He had come to realise that if those in positions of power tell us something often enough and with great certainty, then people believe them. He remembered reading an article on the Masi tribe's view of the UK's handling of the foot and mouth disease in 2001. To them cows are sacred creatures and when their cattle contract foot and mouth, they look after them until they get better – as indeed at least 95% of them do. The article emphasised that there is no reason to slaughter cows and sheep who have foot and mouth. That only the old and weak usually die and the rest recover full health. And yet most people believe otherwise. One of many examples of mass conditioning to which he had been awakened.

Lise had left his life as mysteriously as she had appeared. When she believed that she had completed her work with him she simply disappeared. He had thought that on occasions he had caught a fleeting glimpse of her in various locations, but he couldn't be sure. He still turns to her for answers, or at least considers what her answer would be to an issue with which he is struggling.

His awakening had been painful in many ways, and still was. He had come to realise how much of his life and the lives of others were ruled by fear, and how our society and systems fuelled that fear. Fear of debt, fear of illness, fear of injury, fear of failure, fear of catastrophe and so it goes on, with of course fear of death being the ultimate scaremonger. He had realised that the reason he had driven himself to apparent success was through his fear of failure, fear of loss of face, and fear of being seen by others not to be good enough. Lise had helped to bring this awareness to his consciousness. He wasn't sure now who he really was, in fact he'd never stopped to think about it before. Too busy making his way in the cut throat world of business, to wonder why such a dreadful term as 'cut throat' was used in a business context in the first place. More language which sustains a constant background of fear. "Oh God" he had thought when he recalled some of his own language, "If we don't show significant improvements in performance, heads will roll," "Heads will roll!" Was I about to execute my people?

At least he could smile about it; the fact that he was no longer caught up completely in the trap. He was continually aware that he had much work to do on releasing his deep-held fears and anxieties and in seeking out the self behind the masks and the armour.

At times he had almost found himself overwhelmed with sadness at the way in which we abused ourselves, each other and our planet. We have become consumed by self-indulgence and greed which seemed to be spiralling out of control, he had thought.

He had also often wondered if he could re-access the magical powers that he seemed to possess when he was with Lise, especially the ability to know what people were thinking. He had certainly opened up to his intuitive self and did not now rely only on the logical and rational information available to him.

He had travelled far in many ways since these days and since the proposed take-over of 'Guardian Angel'…

Chapter Two

Take-over

"It's the first of all problems for a man to find out what kind of work he is to do in this universe."

Thomas Carlyle

Douglas sat back and swung his chair away from his desk, full of the new processes and procedures that 'Guardian Angel' had to implement as part of the take-over agreement imposed upon them by their new masters.

As he gazed out of the window his mind was filled with 'what ifs.' What if he had met Lise earlier and had been able to spot the dangers that lay ahead. Those, which had taken away his means of truly influencing 'Guardian Angel.' What if he had acted quicker to put a halt to the process. What if he had dug his heels in and refused to compromise. All hypothetical questions, he could hear Lise tell him; now he had to deal with his present moment challenges.

Douglas, however, still found it difficult not to blame himself for not moving faster in his bid to stay independent. He had spent many sleepless nights going over and over in his mind the possible actions he could have taken. What annoyed him most was that the desire to be bought out had been fuelled by his and others greed to get a bigger slice of the cake. He took a deep breath and released an audible and protracted sigh.

"No shortage of reading material these days!" Bett had first knocked on his door and had come in carrying a large pile of documents.

"More?" Douglas sighed.

"Afraid so Mr Murray – mostly more of what you're going through just now."

"They could start a new industry in their own right and call it something like 'Processes and Procedures Inc.' 'Something for Everyone,' and 'Everything!' How am I actually supposed to run this part of the business and take notice of all this nonsense?"

Bett rolled her eyes and with a resigned look on her face turned and walked out.

* * *

Douglas had eventually decided to attempt to abort the take-over by Universal Bank Inc. and recalled to himself the ensuing boardroom battle which he eventually, and probably inevitably, lost.

"Are you crazy?" John Bell his Chairman had asked, his voice filled with both anger and amazement. "We've been working on this take over for many months. You've been leading our negotiations with my support, and now you say you want to pull out. This is total madness Douglas!"

"It may seem madness to you John, but it now appears to me to be in the best interests of the business, and especially our people, to remain independent. We can then carry on genuinely building the business through our people."

As he spoke, Douglas had taken in the body language and non-verbal responses from his boardroom colleagues. They looked blankly at him, in that incredulous way which people do when they have no sympathy for a point of view. He could see they were stuck in the same world he had inhabited for most of his working life. He couldn't blame them. But for his encounter with Lise, he would still have been sharing that world with them. They had already calculated the likely financial benefits they would accrue from the take-over, and genuinely believed in the myth that 'Guardian Angel' could not continue to grow and develop without becoming part of a large banking empire.

Douglas had asked for more time to finalise his alternative strategy, but this was again met with unanimous resistance.

"We don't have that time available Douglas. Universal are planning to announce the deal by the end of the month, in two weeks time. All we can do is ensure that you are as happy as possible with your role in the new expanding business. Remember also that it was you who initiated the process."

"Touché," Douglas thought, but he still did not capitulate. "We all have the right to change our minds do we not? As you know, I have come to realise that we have the potential within ourselves to continue to expand and develop the business from within. I have shown you the progress we've made over a relatively short period of time through changes we've made in management styles and our culture. Our results are up, our colleague satisfaction ratings are up, our standing in the market place has risen. These are facts you cannot deny."

"We certainly can't deny them," John Bell paused and made fleeting eye contact with each board member except Douglas, "but we can't be sure that this is directly related to your recent changes. We would probably have achieved these results without them, such has the market been of late."

Douglas had begun some time ago to sympathise with the role of what was still called Human Resources – although plans were afoot to rename this key business function at 'Guardian Angel' – in that there was seldom, if ever, any real credit given to any people initiative that could have impacted on sales figures or profit levels. When sales or profits went up, it was mainly credited to upturns in the market. When the market looked to be slowing down, then most people development activities were abandoned to save on costs. It was a 'no win' scenario. Douglas had seen for himself the impact of the development activity he had initiated and could see no sense in withdrawing these if the market did slow down.

Douglas could see he was fighting a losing battle. He did work non-stop for several days to complete his alternative strategy document, but the Board voted overwhelmingly to go ahead with the take-over.

Douglas was allowed some concessions, whilst having to accept that 'Guardian Angel' would lose its true identity, if not its name, and become a small cog in a large bureaucratic, procedure-run company.

* * *

"You couldn't have done any more than you did Douglas. The momentum of the take-over was too great for you to stop." Pat, Douglas's wife, sipped her coffee and sat down beside him. Douglas had been in contemplative mood, considering his options, considering his life ahead.

"I know, but it still hurts deep inside me," he said, "I now have to make some important decisions for myself. Do I stay on now and see how much I can still change at 'Guardian Angel,' or do I look for fresh challenges?" A wave of sadness and panic swept through Douglas as he thought of leaving the business which had been his life for so long. Pat suspected she saw a small tear in the corner of his eye, but didn't comment on it.

"I'm not sure I can work now within a business that has no core values. Admittedly they have a set of what they call 'values', but there are no indications that they understand them, or understand how to work through them. There are no indications either among their people that they are working through any shared values." Douglas was in full flow and regaining his spirit as he expounded elements of his new thinking. "There's also no vision beyond accumulation, no real sense of community, no bigger purpose. I know that what I'm saying probably describes the way most large corporations, and some smaller ones are run, and I'm just not sure now whether I want to be involved if I can't change it."

Pat had seen significant changes in Douglas since his encounters with Lise, not the least being his willingness to trust his intuition.

"What is your gut feeling on what to do?"

"I'll probably have a look firstly at what can be done within 'Guardian Angel,' but ultimately I believe that my future lies elsewhere." He again felt a sense of anxiety deep in the pit of his stomach.

Chapter Three

On the Move!

"What is the use of running if we are on the wrong road?"

Bavarian Proverb

This is the last straw, Douglas thought. The CEO of the new enlarged Universal Bank, Allan Naysmith, had just informed him that the H.R. function was to be centralised within the head office in London with 'Guardian Angel' only having a small number of administrators reporting into the London office. They had already centralised almost all other functions – as he knew they would, but he had been assured by Allan at the time of the take-over that they would still have control over the H.R. policy including, as Douglas saw it, the development he had already initiated. He had, as expected, argued his case with great skill and eloquence, but to no avail. He realised then that his worst fears were becoming a reality and his influence over the future development of 'Guardian Angel' would be minimal.

"This could be seen as constructive dismissal." Douglas challenged Allan Naysmith.

"There's no agenda on our part to get rid of you

Douglas. We know how well you understand the business and especially your own baby, 'Guardian Angel.'"

"You've pretty well decimated what we had created- it's hardly recognisable as my baby as you call it."

"You still have influence over some key elements, and you do have the potential to influence the company as a whole. You're still a relatively young man and your prospects within Universal could be pretty good."

Not in a million years do I want that, Douglas thought, smiling to himself as he remembered how Lise had been able to read his thoughts. Just as well Allan can't do the same. He, however, had become increasingly conscious that he could be pretty well sure of what people were thinking – not absolutely specifically, but enough to make his decisions easier. And he knew Allan didn't mean what he had just said. But in the moment of that internal response he realised that his mind was made up. Staying at Guardian Angel was not an option.

"You know Allan this is one of the saddest periods of my life, and certainly the saddest and most disappointing of my business career."

Allan Naysmith looked at him in amazement "We've just given you a twenty five percent increase in your salary, generous stock options, a superb pension scheme, as well as your choice of executive car, and you say this is the saddest day of your business career."

"You've hit the nail right on the head Allan. Your measures of success are purely financial; your goal in business and in life is 'accumulation' – accumulation of wealth for the few fortunate ones among us who find themselves in these positions. 'Guardian Angel' was more than accumulation. Not always, I admit. It's only in the recent past that I have awakened to the paucity of spirit and community within our business life. If you really looked Allan, you would have seen the strong sense of community and purpose that we were developing within 'Guardian Angel.' You would have been aware of our core values and vision for the business and for the people who worked with us. With some real foresight, Universal could have recognised these strengths and built its future around them. Unfortunately, I have been unable to influence yourself and your colleagues that this was the way to go, and as a result we have followed the 'more of the same' route."

Wow! Douglas felt better for that – as if a weight had been lifted from his chest. He even found himself smiling at Allan.

"Are you saying you can't work with us, Douglas?"

"I'm saying I have grave doubts about whether I can continue in my current role, but would like a little time to think it over."

"I can't give you more than a few weeks at the most. If you're not going to be with us we really need to get someone in place as soon as possible. If it leaks out it could do us serious damage – the city won't like the uncertainty."

"I'll let you know within two weeks – at the end of the month."

"That's fine." Allan stuck out his hand, shook hands, turned and walked out of Douglas's office.

Douglas knew he had made up his mind but wanted a little breathing space to plan his future.

* * *

"I need to open the door." Douglas was quite breathless as he almost jogged along the corridor.

"What door?" Pat asked, as she caught up with him from behind.

"Moving!" Douglas felt exasperated as he had expected to find the door before now and the corridor seemed never ending. "Moving what, where?" Pat remained calm and logical as ever. "Moving On! That's it there." Douglas pointed excitedly at the dark green door with the words 'MOVING ON.com' painted in large white letters.

"Lets go!" Douglas then threw his hands up with delight and woke up with a start with a throbbing hand which he had banged against the bed head in his excitement. He lay on his back recalling the door and the lettering 'MOVING ON.com' obviously a result of his meeting with Allan Naysmith and his decision to leave 'Guardian Angel.' He turned over and was asleep again in minutes.

Chapter Four

New Mysteries

"If at first the idea is not absurd, then there is no hope for it."

Albert Einstein

Douglas sighed once again as he sat down at his desk. The mound of bureaucratic garbage seemed to be never ending. Douglas had risen earlier than usual, unable to get "MOVING ON.com' from his mind. He kept getting flashes of the dark green door with the white lettering. What was behind the door he wondered, and smiled as this in turn reminded him of the famous Elvis Presley song. Amazing how the mind made these connections he thought, and how a sense of humour kept things light. Something he had always possessed and which Lise had rekindled. He found it quite easy to poke fun at himself now, whereas in the recent past his ego made sure that business issues were never a laughing matter.

He switched on his pc to check his emails which had increased four fold since the take-over by Universal. Just as he had persuaded his team and the business as a whole to reduce the number of emails they sent, they were once again overwhelmed by mostly pointless emails from people 'copying him in' probably to protect their rear ends as they saw it. Oops! Douglas had clicked on the wrong icon and had accessed the Internet. Why not? he thought, as he typed in www.MOVINGON.com and waited for the inevitable 'address unknown.' Instead, and to his amazement, the address was being accessed. Douglas could feel his heart pounding in his chest and noticed that his mouth had become dry. The site was appearing as a dark green background with a quote written in white lettering…

"It takes a lot of courage to release the familiar, and seemingly secure, to embrace the new. But there is no real security in what is no longer meaningful. There is more security in the adventurous and exciting, for in movement there is life, and in change there is power."
Alan Cohen

Douglas stared at the screen in disbelief. Underneath the quote it said…

'Time to move.., no time to lose, see you at your next stop.'

As he finished reading the message the words faded out and were replaced by a mountain scene on web-cam. Snow capped peaks plunging down into lush green valleys carved in two by a fast flowing powerful river that sparkled in what looked like early morning sunshine. Douglas took a deep breath as he took in both the serenity and the power of the scene- a place to uplift and inspire. Truly amazing he thought. So that's what was going on behind the green door he laughed to himself. And a message from Lise he was sure.

"No time to lose – more work to do!" He could feel the excitement welling up inside and his spirits lifting. He shook his head again, he couldn't stop shaking it nor could he stop smiling. He had no idea where his next 'stop' would be, but he had faith that it would be the right one. There certainly was more work to be done, all he needed at the moment was the right vehicle.

Chapter Five

The End In Sight

*"We must always change, renew, regenerate ourselves;
otherwise we harden."*

Goethe

Two days later the phone rang in Douglas's office. It was Bett phoning through from her office. "I have a gentleman on the line who wants to speak with you. Says it's very important, but won't give his name. Will you take the call?"

This guy must have done a superb selling job on Bett, as it was very rare that she would put a call through without knowing who the caller was or why he or she was phoning.

Douglas wasn't going to miss out on anything at that moment. "Sure, put him through."

"Good morning Mr Murray," the voice on the end of the phone was very smooth and cultured. A headhunter without a doubt, thought Douglas.

"My name is Ian Home. I'm a partner in the recruitment firm of Home and Garden."

Douglas could barely suppress his laughter.

"I have an opportunity which I think may be of interest to you. I hear on the grapevine that you may be considering a move."

"That's news to me," Douglas reckoned on giving nothing away until he was sure who the caller was. "What grapevine are you using these days?" Douglas laughed.

"Yes indeed Mr Murray, our grapevines are complex networks. Never quite sure where a story starts."

Goodish answer, thought Douglas.

"Can you give me some details of your business to confirm to me that you are a head hunter."

"Yes, of course. We've been in business now for twelve years specialising in recruiting in the financial services sector. We have pitched a few times for your business when you were independent. I can give you contact names if you wish."

"No, no, I don't think that would be a great idea. I haven't taken action to move job, but I would be interested at least to see what you have to offer." Douglas hugely understated his response, when in fact he was desperate to hear what Ian Home had to offer.

"Why don't we meet to discuss the position?"

"That would suit me," Douglas said "Somewhere discreet I suggest."

"I'll book a meeting room at the Hilton Hotel which is close by your office. Tomorrow good for you?"

After finalising the arrangements to meet, Douglas opened his cv file on his pc. He had been working on it discreetly over the past few weeks. Things were definitely moving – a message from Lise with the chance he may meet her again, and a job interview lined up for the next day.

One key task he would have to complete was his list of conditions any business would have to comply with in order for him to consider taking the post.

Douglas's meeting the following day had gone well. The company in question who were looking to recruit a new Chief Executive was 'Silver Waters Investment', a boutique financial services and investment business. The previous incumbent had been in post for three years and had agreed when he took the position that he would move on at that point. From the information Douglas was shown, the business was shaping up well with a strong balance sheet, a sizeable level of funds under management, and a good name in the market place. He had, of course, heard of them and had been impressed with their performance as a relative newcomer to the scene, as well as also liking their name. It was a company that Douglas could see himself running.

He handed over the more detailed investigation into 'Silver Waters' to his lawyer and accountant, while he got down to drawing up his requirements as CEO. He also intended meeting with as big a cross section of people as possible in the circumstances to get a feel for the culture of the business.

Since his meeting and work with Lise, Douglas had been drawn to a whole new range of reading material. His norm had been business books and novels when on holiday. Subsequently, he had been introduced to books such as 'Way of the Peaceful Warrior' by Dan Millman and 'The Celestine Prophecy' by James Redfield and other popular, – what some people referred to – as new age books. Recently he had dipped into a range of titles that took him further into the fields of shamanism, healing and mysticism. His initial aim was to make more sense of his experience with Lise, which he had realised, had been a healing experience for himself and subsequently for his people.

He often laughed to himself when he thought of what the 'old' Douglas would have made of that.

"A load of old ...!" probably.

He had been fascinated with the initial insights Lise had given him into how other cultures made sense of their world – how, for example, the indigenous Guatemalans sustained their communities through 'built-in inefficiencies', never building houses to last too long, so that when they reached a state of collapse the community rebuilt the houses and the community at the same time. Douglas wondered if he could introduce an element of this in his new company if he was offered, and accepted, the position.

He had become increasingly frustrated by the culture in the West of revering people who became millionaires, and paying homage to them on television programmes like 'Mind of a Millionaire' of which he had caught a glimpse sometime ago on the BBC. Their focus had been on entrepreneurs who had accumulated various levels of fortunes. The presenter referred to the millionaires as wealth creators. But Douglas begged to differ – we're talking stockpiling wealth generally for the benefit of either one, or a few individuals. We're talking exploiting child / cheap labour in the East, Douglas said to himself. We're talking low paid jobs, and in many cases lifeless working environments in the UK. Even worse in Douglas's view was one of the entrepreneur's beliefs that you have to "hate your competitors." Wow! If there wasn't enough of that going round in the world as it was without business people adding to it. Douglas was on his metaphorical soapbox which always stimulated him into thinking of ways to avoid being caught up in traps.

He knew that he was part of a privileged elite of people who ran medium to large sized companies, were paid large salaries with lots of perks and would never, unless they were very reckless, find themselves in serious financial difficulties. What he was determined to do was use his privilege to good effect. To run a business which was financially successful, had a dynamic and energetic culture where everyone could contribute, and which recognised its responsibility to the wider community both at home and abroad. A pretty good personal mission statement, he thought, but he also realised he had a good deal of work still to do on himself as part of the process.

Chapter Six

"A New Beginning"

"We are in this world for an adventure of personal growth and positive contribution"

Tom Morris

Douglas had spent some time, firstly thinking through his requirements for his potential new position, and then compiling them for presentation. Salary and perks weren't really a concern. He would be more or less remunerated similarly to his current job in Universal. What he wanted to be sure of was his breadth of control and influence. He knew, of course, that he would have to work through a Board of Directors, but would want full operational autonomy to implement his own ideas and he hoped, those of his colleagues.

He didn't really anticipate any great difficulty in convincing the Board about his plans. They would probably be pretty sceptical about him being able to implement them anyway. They would be more concerned with his financial housekeeping at 'Guardian Angel' and whether the City would approve of his appointment. The 'City', thought Douglas, the all-powerful City. We'd soon have to ask them permission to get a haircut or even go to the toilet! He laughed to himself at the thought. What annoyed Douglas were these jumped up twenty-something City analysts who spouted off about the management ability in a company when they had never been anywhere near a management job in their life. What was more depressing was that people actually listened to them, and believed them. On such flimsy opinions could a company's share price fall dramatically, and even worse.

Coming off his soapbox. Douglas began putting his thoughts on paper. He would, of course, work with his new Management Team on all aspects of business development and would expect all to take a full part in the process, though Douglas believed that a key role as Chief Executive was for him to articulate his vision of the business's future. This could be embellished and modified to some extent through dialogue with his team, but he really believed it was his ultimate responsibility to initiate the vision, to be a visionary leader. So one of his first tasks would be to agree and articulate a shared vision for the company. He would ensure that this was specific and practical enough for people to understand and be inspired by. It would encompass both the external and internal measures of success. In fact 'success' as a concept was something he intended exploring with his new team. He thought that would be a good starting point in their work together. He made a note to do some background research into writers on the subject of 'success'. He intended presenting his vision of an open style culture with an enabling style of management which would invite contributions from every area of the business.

He wondered about introducing his ideas on new business terminology – colleagues instead of staff or employees etc. but reckoned that was a step too far at this time. Lise had convinced him well on the need for establishing core values that people could understand and work through. He had seen the difference this had made at 'Guardian Angel,' where there was now much greater consistency and congruency in decision making, management style and focus. There was greater clarity all round as people could understand the reason for decisions or actions taken, and much more energy going towards making things happen than complaining about why they had to be done.

He would give one or two examples to emphasise the importance he placed on these. More importantly though, he would have to sell the fact that the Board would also have to work through these values to make decision making consistent throughout the business. There is no benefit in operational managers working through shared core values if the decisions from the Board cut across these, or pay no attention to them. A factor which ultimately leads to cynicism and lack of focus. This could be the most challenging task for him, he thought. Probably not in getting the job, more when he was in situ. It was, therefore, vital that they were aware of his plans at the outset.

These he felt were the key factors to be covered, with the overall expectation that the Board would stick to strategic matters and leave him free rein to build and develop the internal strength of the company.

Douglas had already done some background research on the company and how it had been run. Their promotional material presented an image of a modern, go ahead, innovative business looking to stand out from the crowd in as many ways as possible. They had won a number of business awards over the years, including 'Best Newcomer,' 'Fastest Grower,' 'Best Employer' amongst others. The latter awards had impressed Douglas as an indicator that they could be on the same wavelength as him.

The recruitment process went very smoothly. He had informal interviews with the Chairman, Alex King, two Executive Directors and two Non-Executive Directors. Encouragingly, one of the Executive Directors and one of the Non-Executive Directors were women. A good start, he had thought. This was followed by a more formal process where he had to make a detailed presentation to the Board and then be grilled for an hour and a half with questions from all members. He had been a little nervous before he started but had enjoyed himself once he got going. It felt good to be moving again – in a sense it didn't matter whether he got the job, he was pleased to be involved.

Douglas needn't have worried anyway. The Board members were apparently very impressed with him – he was basically the person they wanted ever since they heard on the grapevine that he might be available. They had been surprised by Douglas's interest in developing the corporate culture and in his commitment to core values, but they didn't consider this to be a problem. Most of them had appeared to agree with him when he declared that their decision making would also need to be guided by these values.

Ian Home phoned him two days after his presentation, apologised for taking so long to get back to him, and told him he had been offered the post of Chief Executive of 'Silver Waters Investments.'

Douglas said he would be delighted to accept the offer but would wait until he had received the offer in writing before resigning his current position. The reports he had received from his lawyers and accountants had been favourable. He liked what he had seen of the business, so he was happy indeed to move on.

The formalities hadn't taken long. He had received the formal offer the next day. He and his lawyer had gone through it carefully before Douglas signed it. He then contacted the CEO of Universal, met with him the following day and handed him his letter of resignation. Allan Naysmith had said all the right things about him being sorry that he couldn't have stayed, that he was sure the company would continue to benefit from the work he had put in, and so on. Douglas felt as if he was in a dream. He didn't really hear Allan Naysmith's words. The whole episode had felt unreal, partly he felt because he probably had never imagined he would ever leave his 'baby', 'Guardian Angel.' But the reality was that this was it! He was relieved to leave the building and took a deep breath of fresh air as he stepped outside and effectively into a new life.

Universal released the news to the press the following day, with an accompanying piece released by 'Silver Waters.' Two articles, and two photographs in the paper on the same day. Douglas had been quietly amused.

Back in his office he had been clearing his desk and contemplating his future. Sadness mixed with excitement. The Alan Cohen quote on that web site had really prevented him from becoming over reflective and melancholic about his move but he had been having recurring dreams about doors that had unsettled him – yes, these doors again! Sometimes he would get to the door and it would disappear. Or, on other occasions, he got to the door and it just would not open, and the previous night he had managed to get the door to open a few inches and then it jammed. He just could not figure out what this all meant. Was there a deeper meaning to these dreams he wondered?

"What would you be thinking if you were the door?"

Douglas shook his head wondering what a weird question to ask. Then he almost fell out of his chair as he swung round in amazement, eyes popping out of his head. He tried to speak but couldn't get any words out. Emotion welled up inside him.

"Where the hell did you come from?" realising what a stupid question it was as he asked it.

Lise was standing in front of his desk smiling at him as she had done when they had met for the first time. Although their usual greeting had always previously been a handshake, Douglas on this occasion came round from behind his desk, stood in front of her for a moment to make sure this wasn't a dream, before giving her a lengthy hug.

"So you are pleased to see me? I did wonder." she looked at Douglas with an impish grin on her face.

"Sit down, sit down." Douglas was quite away with himself. He had never really been much of a hugger, but had no hesitation on this occasion. He was pulling a chair across for Lise, whilst trying surreptitiously to wipe away a tear from his eye, again knowing that Lise would notice this anyway.

"Well," she said, "What would you be thinking if

you were the door?" It was as if she had never been away.

"Can I just have a moment to settle and reconnect before going into class!" Douglas laughed.

"Of course, but only a moment!" she laughed with him.

"Where have you been? You just disappeared. I couldn't find any contact address or phone number for you."

"I had completed my work with you at that time and you needed to deal with what was happening by yourself. You had to make your own decisions based on your own developing awareness, using your re-discovered intuition along the way."

"Mmm, I can see your point, but there were several moments when I could have done with your help."

"And you didn't get it?" Lise teased him. Douglas nodded his head in appreciation. "You've had a busy time of it these past few months and you're finally moving on. Pleased?"

"Sad, but relieved I've made the decision. Knowing what I now know, I couldn't have stayed with 'Guardian Angel.' There's a strong likelihood also that the name will soon disappear and that 'Universal' will sell off the parts they don't see as profitable enough or that don't fit with their image. It's my colleagues I feel sadness for, with a future of fear and uncertainty. Always fear involved somewhere along the line. You know my new Chairman at 'Silver Waters.' – what a great name for a company, don't you think?" Lise nodded her approval "– spoke with me earlier today to say, 'wouldn't it be a good idea to make our first exercise together a SWOT analysis.' You know, identify your

Strengths, Weaknesses, Opportunities and Threats. Can you spot the fear-based elements? I said I would like to talk this over with him before going ahead, as I had one or two suggestions to make."

"For example?" Lise was back into quizzical mode, "and," she added "I haven't forgotten about the door either!"

"Well, I had always accepted these so called business tools like SWOT analysis or SMART goals as legitimate business aids, until I began to waken up and wonder why we want to spend time reviewing our Weaknesses, and more particularly, start frightening ourselves with potential Threats. Oh, I know the business schools will tell me that you have to be aware of your weaknesses, and I say 'why?' – it reminds me of my parents telling me to make sure I knew my limitations! And 'Threats?' I'm not sure who thought that one up."

"Any alternatives?"

"Yes – simply miss these two factors out and focus on our Strengths and the Opportunities available to us. The first shows us where we can do our best work, where our true talents lie, and inspire us with this awareness, and the second can cover our need to develop new strengths, as well as seek out new opportunities in the market place. This keeps our current energy high while remaining focused on how we can develop in the future. What do you think?"

Lise clapped when Douglas finished. "It sounds good to me. Couldn't have told it better myself. Now, how about this door?"

"What was it you asked me again, I know it was a weird question?"

"What would you be thinking if you were the door?"

"It is a great question. What a gift to ask such great questions!"

"What would I be thinking if I was the door?" Douglas repeated the question out loud.

"I'd be wondering why this guy was always wanting to open me to find out what was on the other side. I'd be thinking he showed great perseverance in continually coming back to try again."

"What about his strategy?"

"What do you mean his strategy?"

"What he was doing to get to the other side of the door."

"Yes, I could be wondering why he hadn't thought of other ways of opening the door."

"Like what?"

Douglas remembered then how persistent Lise was in challenging him to think.

"Like break it down, blow it up, although neither very environmentally friendly."

"What if the door could talk?" Lise was pleased to be back helping Douglas to see the unusual.

"Doors can't talk though."

"It's a dream, Douglas, a dream! And maybe the door is a metaphor. What do you think?"

"Ok, so the door can talk." Douglas laughed – a little bit at his lack of insight.

"Be kind to yourself." Lise reminded him.

"So if the door can talk, I could ask it why it didn't want to open."

"And the corollary of that."

"Of course, I could ask it to open, or what I needed to do to get it to open."

They both sighed and smiled at his eventual discovery.

"Next time you have the dream, and if you can

become conscious as you dream, talk to the door. You may even discover what it really represents to you. You have without doubt opened many doors since we first met. And there's more to come!"

"So will you be staying on this time around?"

"For a while, I think. Could be fun with new challenges ahead."

"Do you want to work at 'Silver Waters,' or I could employ you as a consultant?"

"A consultant indeed!" Lise laughed as she sat up very straight with a self-important look on her face.

"Let's take it a step at a time. We can look again once you're in your new post."

Chapter Seven

"First Encounter"

"All work is empty save when there is love, for work is love made visible."

Kahil Gibran

Douglas had not been required to work his notice at 'Guardian Angel.' The company had given him a week to sort things out before he moved out. He took a week off to re-orientate himself before starting with 'Silver Waters.' He had spent the week around the house reading and relaxing and, of course, walking his beloved dog Tara. Pat had been amazed to hear of Lise's return, although Douglas had noticed a little reticence over how she might work with Douglas in the future. Three days or so had been quite acceptable. The possibility of a longer term working relationship wasn't as appealing for her. Douglas had told her that they hadn't decided on how they would work together, for all he knew, he said, she might disappear again. Pat hoped that would be the case, but didn't come out and say it. It was a difficult one. Douglas obviously wanted to benefit from Lise's insights, but couldn't see what role she could be given. The CEO's personal guru or shaman he had joked. But, as Lise had said, this could be sorted out in time.

Douglas had noticed himself once again getting trapped into left brain thinking – having to know what was going to happen. He recalled Lise's explanation of Outcome and Process, and agreed to stay in the Process, and enjoy the journey.

He had begun planning his first management team meeting that he had arranged for nine o'clock on the first Tuesday in his new post. He had indicated that he had expected all team members to be present.

He had inherited a team of five senior managers. Stewart Price was Finance Director and also a member of the Board. Louise Sanders was his Marketing Director and Pete Fisher his HR Director. One of his early challenges would be to agree a new name for HR – if he was stuck on HR they could always compromise by calling it the Human Relations Team. That was another goal – getting rid of 'Departments' and renaming them Teams. He knew some people would consider it a cosmetic or trendy exercise, but he understood the power of language and would aim to persuade others of its significance.

Mark Adams was his Business Development Director and Joan Stevens was Head of Investments. He would review their roles in time and look at whether he might add to his team. On first meeting they had all appeared capable experienced people willing to welcome Douglas into the business. Douglas had hoped that his nickname of 'Deadly Doug' would not follow him into his new company.

As well as asking each of his Team to provide a short presentation on the current work of their teams, he had also asked them to prepare a short piece on their perception of success – how they would measure success at 'Silver Waters.' He reckoned that this would give him a good feel for some of their values. He would deal with core values at subsequent meetings. He also planned to start out as he intended to continue with the format of meetings, and had a few ideas he would introduce progressively over the first few weeks.

There were a few interesting and questioning looks on the faces of his team as they walked into the meeting room on Tuesday morning. And one or two wry smiles.

Firstly the ubiquitous board room type table was conspicuous by its absence, leaving a small semi-circle of chairs. Mark Adams was wondering where he could put his laptop so that he could get on with his work if the topic in question didn't relate to him as he saw it!

That wasn't all. On a table at the top of the room was a magnificent arrangement of fresh flowers, the scent of which filled the room.

Douglas had thought about having some relaxing or meditational music on when they came in and had decided to introduce that at a subsequent meeting.

He had been in the room to meet and greet each team member as they entered, and they had the choice of tea, coffee or freshly squeezed fruit juices to set the ball rolling.

Douglas had started the meeting by indicating that this format was only the start and that the aim would be to ensure that their meetings were purposeful and enjoyable. He also welcomed their ideas and inputs to developing team meetings and to building a strong team ethos.

The next part of the meeting was an opportunity for Douglas to hear each team member's update on their area of work. A pretty standard approach at these meetings he had thought, but he needed this information and he was keen to observe how each of his colleagues approached their task. They had all been fairly well prepared, some more so than others. All came across as knowledgeable and interested in their work and in the business.

Douglas had thanked them for their presentations and moved on to his team's perception of success.

"Before we begin," Joan Stevens had said, "Can you please say a few words about the purpose of this exercise?"

"Yes, of course." Douglas wasn't surprised that someone had asked him the question, and had prepared his answer.

"I wanted to observe the similarities and potential differences across the team in relation to what each of you is aiming for. It will also give each of us some understanding of what motivates us. I also wanted to complete this before we do any work together around our shared vision and core values."

Pete Fisher perked up when he heard these last two concepts mentioned. "Does that seem fair?" He looked firstly at Joan who nodded and smiled and then made eye contact with each of his remaining colleagues. Each indicated they were happy to move on.

* * *

"So these are the outcomes from our discussions on 'Success.'" Douglas had been in his office later in the day when Lise had slipped in briefly for a chat.

"I know," she raised her eyebrows and smiled.

"Well let's review them anyway."

Douglas had formatted them on power point and projected them to the screen at the back of his office.

'Steady, Year on Year business growth,
with a well managed cost base'

"No prizes for guessing that's from the Finance Director." Douglas laughed.

'Outstripping our competitors on all competitive
indicators and where possible taking
business from them'

"Louise Saunders, Marketing."

'Being the best in our sector,
being seen to be the best.'

"HR?" Lise asked.
"Yes, that's Pete Fisher."

'All measurable areas of our business
to be over-performing.'

"Joan Stevens, Investment."
"And…"

'Consistently over achieving on financial targets.'

"From Mark Adams, Business Development."
"What are your thoughts?"
"I truly wonder why you had to ask!"
"Well, you may have changed them. It does sometimes happen."
"I would say the responses were as expected – very business-like and very traditional."
"Is that some kind of euphemism for something else you wanted to say?" She smiled.

"I suppose I am a bit disappointed, but not surprised. They are all relatively young people operating in a young company and yet their model of the business world is pretty much the same as the models that have been kicking around for a century or more. Will I be able to change these? That's my challenge. To be able to create the type of organisation I had begun to develop at 'Guardian Angel,' where success is a more expansive and encompassing concept."

Lise noticed that Douglas's energy level had dropped. He looked tired, even a little depressed she thought. He was sitting looking at the ground – a most unlikely pose for Douglas.

"You all right?" she asked, putting her hand on his shoulder. He lifted his head slowly and took a deep breath.

"It's been a tough time for me over the past few months. It feels as if I'm starting from scratch again with yet another mountain to climb."

"Perhaps you need a break to re-energise and re-focus."

"Pat and I had a break a couple of months ago. A week in the sun in Cannes."

* * *

"Maybe you need a different kind of break. An experience that will challenge and invigorate you at the same time. Something which will stimulate your creative juices and expand your mind."

Douglas was looking at the ground again, deep in thought. Something he had seen recently had both inspired him and excited thoughts of travel, but he couldn't remember what it was.

"Mmm, just trying to remember something." he

said quietly. He then stood up and stretched himself with his hands above his head and strolled over to the window for inspiration. Lise left him in his contemplation, whilst knowing exactly what was going on. She was a bit worried about him. She hadn't seen him as quiet or as tired as he appeared to be.

"Got it!" Lise jumped a little as Douglas turned around with a gleeful look on his face.

"I remember now." Douglas looked more animated than before. "It was that amazing scene that appeared on the web site after your message disappeared. Magnificent mountains, with what looked like a series of terraces at various locations, with a majestic river splitting lush fertile valleys."

While Douglas had been busy eulogising on this great place he had found, Lise had been quietly accessing the Internet on his laptop.

"Is this what you're talking about?" she said swivelling the screen round towards Douglas.

"Wow! A thousand times wow!" Douglas sat down gazing at the screen. "Any idea where it is?"

"It's Peru" Lise replied.

"Peru! It looks fabulous."

"That's the Urambamba River you see and hear as it tumbles its way towards the Amazon."

"And the mountains are the Andes, I presume?" Douglas couldn't take his eyes off the scene, which was once again being relayed by web cam. He didn't ask how or why. The remarkable was always present where Lise was concerned.

"Yes that's right, and I do agree they are magnificent."

Douglas sat shaking his head in what looked to Lise like apparent disbelief.

"Yes?" she enquired of him.

"In the past – in pre-Lise days," Douglas grinned, "I would have been amazed at the apparent coincidences that appeared to be occurring around Peru."

"In what way?" Lise leaned back and folded her arms in a mock teacher like action.

"Well, I've not long finished reading the 'Celestine Prophecy' which is based in Peru, and I've just completed 'The Eagle's Quest' by Fred Alan Wolfe, part of which is also based in Peru. He recounts his experience with the jungle shamans of Peru and his initiation into the use of ayahuasca as a vehicle for personal transformation."

"I'm familiar with the 'Celestine Prophecy' which is, of course, a fictional tale providing nine insights into life, but have not come across 'The Eagles Quest.' Tell me more."

"Fred Alan Wolfe is a theoretical physicist who has investigated shamanism from a physicist's point of view. Part of his work was to experience the effects of ayahuasca, a hallucinogenic plant-based substance known as the vision vine. Assisting you in releasing past fears, it takes you into the realm of spirit and opens up pathways for personal growth. He also investigates many other shamanic practices and psychological concepts."

"So what did you mean when you said you would have been amazed at the apparent coincidences?"

"My growing awareness now tells me that I am being attracted towards this material for a reason rather than by chance."

"Or maybe it's being attracted by you!"

"Whatever way it works, Lise, it feels to me that Peru has some significance for me."

"Peru itself or shamanism in Peru?" she asked, wanting to help Douglas clarify in his own mind what he wanted.

"Not absolutely sure on that one. Probably Peru as the prime pull, and, at the moment, shamanism as the secondary draw, although I really feel they go hand-in-hand. "

"And do you see a relationship between your work at 'Silver Waters' and Peru?"

"Not an obvious one at the moment, simply an intuitive sense that there is some important learning to be done there."

"And healing perhaps?" Lise suggested

"Perhaps." Douglas replied absent mindedly not absolutely sure what she meant.

"Think about it, and we can take this further next time if you want." Lise had stood up and was walking towards the door "See you soon."

As she left, Douglas felt a wave of anxiety sweep over him. For the first time in his life he felt really challenged at a personal level. Obviously the 'Guardian Angel' take-over and his subsequent resignation had been traumatic, but now he began, at some level, to doubt himself. Doubt whether he was capable of real change in himself and whether he could effect real change in the business world.

Fear had never been a major element of his life before. He had always felt assured he was on the right path and making steady progress towards a goal. His main frustration then was the apparent lack of interest and real commitment his colleagues had compared to him. 'Only a job' was how he had seen their perception of the job. And then came Lise… who opened his eyes to the part he was playing in this scenario. OK he had initially been a bit cynical and very sceptical, but what she had shown him convinced him that he had been on the wrong track, unaware of how his actions influenced those around him – and not always productively!

The experience had also convinced him that most businesses were on the wrong track. That success could not be judged purely from the standpoint of financial accumulation. He had seen the difference in the performance of his people when he had helped to initiate a more connected, energised culture where everyone was respected and could benefit from the financial success of his business. He smiled when he remembered the response of his Board, who believed his initiatives had not been responsible for the improvement in results. Stuck in their conditioned reality, he thought. Stuck in the past. And now he was facing similar challenges at 'Silver Waters.'

He wondered for a moment if he should have stayed at 'Guardian Angel,' taken the easy route, kept his head down and possibly retired early. He knew deep down though that that was never an option. He had genuinely found something else within himself, possibly had found himself. This thought comforted him as he began to wrestle with his new challenges and with the fear he was now experiencing.

So how would I define success he thought? He started with a mind map.

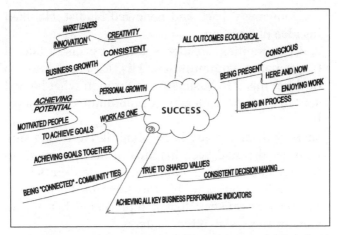

"What will be my key elements?" Douglas had decided previously not to present his concept of success until he had assimilated his colleagues views, and had promised to give his understanding of success at their next meeting. He decided to present it in bullet point form rather than a statement as his team members had done.

Pulling the items from the mind map he started to make a list…

Achieving goals together

Achieving our potential through consistent personal and business growth

Building communities who overcome challenges whilst staying cohesive

Stimulating innovation to become market leaders

Staying true to our shared values and demonstrating consistent decision making

All our achievements are ecological

Have fun! Enjoy work.

Douglas sat back and reviewed his list. He liked his idea of building

Communities, an idea sparked by Lise's tale of Guatemalan communities. His idea on how to develop this into business was through what he had started to call 'Leadership Communities', a concept he wanted to share with Lise, although he more than suspected she already knew about it. He wasn't sure whether this had been his idea or not. He seems to remember something similar in Arie de Geus's book 'The Living Company.' He may fine-tune his list later, but he was satisfied that it represented his overall view of success at 'Silver Waters.'

Chapter Eight

Beyond the Door

"There is no fruit that is not bitter before it is ripe."

Publilius Syrus (85-43BC)

" That door again!" Douglas complained once again frustrated that it was there in the first place, and secondly that he still couldn't get it open. Something stirred inside him however, and he took a step back, sucked in a deep breath and asked in hushed tones "What do I have to do to open you?"

Douglas felt a bit stupid speaking to a door especially with so many people staring at him. What were they doing there anyway, this was his door! He was about to slip away quietly when the door replied

"Why do you want to open me?"

Douglas's mouth opened – something he had got used to with his work with Lise. A talking door, what next he thought grinning to himself. His audience also seemed to find it amusing.

"I want to see what's inside."

"Inside where?"

Douglas seemed to recognise the voice but couldn't exactly place it.

"I want you to open so that I can go onto the other

side, and see what's there."

"You might not like it when you get there!"

My God, I'm now having to rationalise my actions with a door! Douglas couldn't believe it. "I think I'm prepared – I feel I'm ready for anything, and I would be most appreciative if you could now let that happen." He had used the most conciliatory tone he could muster.

"OK, you may enter." and at that moment the door transformed briefly into a mirror which Douglas saw a reflection of himself – except he was dressed in old style clothes much like those he had seen in pictures of Andrew Carnegie, and then disappeared all together leaving an open doorway for Douglas to enter.

He stepped forward tentatively, noticing that his 'audience' had moved away and that it seemed as if the door was an entrance to a cave of some sort.

He sucked in another deep breath and entered. The hairs on the back of his neck were standing to attention and he could feel his heart pounding against his rib cage. He felt a rush of cold air as he entered. It was dark and dank, with a musty smell that comes through lack of ventilation. As he took his first few steps away from the door, he turned round and gasped as the door, or opening as it now appeared to be, closed behind him. He was now shaking with fear. He waited for some moments until his eyes adjusted to the darkness and decided to move on into the cave. Walking was difficult as the floor of the cave was covered in rocks. He moved forward with one careful step at a time, making sure he was balanced before he took his next step.

As he went further into the cave, he could now see that there were piles of waste materials deposited on its floor. Old pieces of metal, machine components, even some clapped-out machines from the past. As he passed close by one he stopped for a moment as he could see 'Made in Scotland' engraved on the side. Many years ago by the looks of it, he muttered to himself.

He could hear running water ahead of him, and as he walked on slowly a little more, he could begin to see the reflection of a fast running stream dancing on the wall of the cave. There must be a light source coming from somewhere he thought as he came closer to the water and noticed it sparkle as it bounced over the rocky floor of the stream.

He took a final careful step bringing both feet together a couple of feet from the edge of the stream. He leant forward slowly, knelt down and put his hand into the water. He could feel the power of the running water against the palm of his hand. Its coolness was a welcome relief. He put both hands in, cupping them together and splashed some water on his face. At least he thought he had, yet he felt no sensation of water at all. He repeated the action and again nothing. The water seemed to evaporate before it could get to his face.

He decided to follow the stream further down into the cave. He took great care in ensuring both feet had a stable base before gingerly standing up again. Ah sh… he couldn't believe it – his right foot simply gave way and he felt himself tumble forward into the stream. As he hit the water on his back, it felt as if he had landed on a soft cushion. Within moments he had been swept down the stream and landed abruptly with a jolt on soft sand. He had closed his eyes initially as he fell, expecting the worst, not sure if he would be knocked unconscious. When he opened them again as he hit the sand, he was now bathed in what appeared like moonlight, and yet he was in the same cave. He stood up and brushed the sand off his clothes, once again amazed that he wasn't wet at all despite having fallen in the stream.

"Welcome Douglas, I've been waiting for you. What took you so long?"

Douglas almost jumped out of his skin. He turned round to see a small, well built but quite squat man coming towards him with his arms outstretched. His skin was brown and hair jet black, with the features of a native South American. He was wearing off-white cotton pants and a light blue loose fitting shirt and sandals. And he was grinning from one side of his large brown face to the other.

"Should I know him?" Douglas wondered as his new found friend approached him. "How would he know me?" Douglas was attempting to hide his confusion when he was consumed in a bear hug. He had just over-come his reticence in hugging Lise, when here he was being hugged by another man, and one he had never met before! Despite this he decided to go with the flow and hug him back.

"I'm Sam." his new hugging friend said as they broke away from each other. "I'm your guide on this special journey. Anything you want to know, just ask."

"But you said you had been waiting for me. How did you know I'd be coming?"

"Ah, that's something I think you would call intuition!"

"And what would you call it Sam?"

"That's a long story and one which doesn't need telling right now." He spoke very good English, with a Spanish accent. "Let's just say I've been working at that kind of stuff for some time now. The important thing for me is that you get full benefit from your trip here – value for money you would call it in business – yes? Except you don't have to pay any money!" Sam laughed heartily and infectiously at his own joke. Douglas was beginning to enjoy himself, still totally unaware of what was happening.

"So where am I, and what am I doing here?" Douglas realised he sounded very businesslike.

"It was you who wanted the door to open!" Sam's laughter again echoed around the cavern as he put his arm round Douglas and started walking slowly away from the edge of the stream and towards another doorway about twenty or so yards away.

"This is a special place where you will be able to view the past, and get some ideas for the future. Perhaps even start making some plans. I believe you want to help your people and your business, to think and act differently, – more productively. Yes?" Sam squeezed Douglas's shoulder as he posed the question.

"Definitely. Also to let people see that a new way isn't 'soft' as many may think. Rather, that by confronting the way we currently do things, and by facing our fears, we can create businesses where success is not solely measured in pound signs."

"Well said!" Sam stopped a few yards from the entrance to another part of this weird place. Fortunately, he had had lots of practice of weird experiences with his work with Lise so this was looking like just another of the same for Douglas.

"I'm about to accompany you on a journey through a series of chambers." Sam had released his arm from around Douglas's shoulder and was now standing beside him pointing towards this entry point.

"Each of the chambers will provide you with insights into organisations past and present. The first is 'The Chamber of Wounds' where you will experience some of the less attractive aspects of organisations' behaviour over the years. I'm not sure exactly what we will see or hear, but I will be happy to answer any questions you may have. Ready?" Sam placed his hand at the base of Douglas's back in anticipation of moving forward.

"Onwards and upwards." Douglas turned smiling at Sam.

"Maybe even onwards and downwards!" Sam's laughter again bounced off the cave walls. As they walked through the doorway they entered a vast arena with a maze-like path winding its way through a variety of different scenarios, almost like mini business units.

"We'll work our way round in a clock-wise direction." Sam led the way to their left and the first scenario.

As they walked in Douglas saw a number of different people as if from different ages. One looked surprising like Scrooge, or how Douglas had imagined him to look. He was, unsurprisingly, counting money into a safe, whilst another of the 'players' was dressed in a beautiful Armani suit and was engrossed with his laptop.

"Can I take a look?" Douglas asked Sam

"Go ahead." Sam stood back to let Douglas walk around behind the man at his computer. "What's he doing?" Sam asked.

"He's working through spread sheets. Looks like sales figures of some kind. Can I ask him a question?"

"Of course." Sam settled down on the edge of the desk to watch.

"Excuse me." Douglas tapped lightly on the man's shoulder. "May I interrupt you for a moment?"

The man turned round to face Douglas, his expression indicating he was less than happy to be disturbed.

"Make it quick then." He showed no emotions.

"What kind of business are you involved in?"

"I'm a serial entrepreneur, mainly in mobile phones and electronic communication systems."

"What's your key purpose in business?" Douglas wanted to make it quick.

"Making money. Simple as that!"

"You mean to say you have no other purpose in business other than to make money?" Douglas pressed on.

"Absolutely not! The business of making money always comes first for me. It's the only way to guarantee success, and it's what the city demands."

He turned back to his laptop, a signal that Douglas took to mean that the conversation was over.

Next in line seemed to be a meeting of some sort in a typical boardroom setting. Douglas walked towards the group and stopped within hearing distance to listen to their conversation. It looked to him to be like many of the meetings he had attended over the years. The participants were all looking very grim faced and worried. The chairperson was addressing the meeting....

"We've known for some time that the results have not been as good as expected this current year, and we have already issued two profits warnings to that effect. What we're looking at is a likely year-end profit of only £450M." Douglas smiled at the use of 'only.'

"But surely that's a pretty good performance? It's £25M up on last year," a younger member of the group interjected.

After a withering look, the chairperson continued.

"We are aware of that John, but it is £50M short of our forecast and the city will not like it. We have to show them that we mean business and are implementing the necessary strategies to recover our position over the coming year. To this effect, I am recommending cutting our workforce by 10% and implementing a raft of cost-cutting initiatives, a copy of which you have in front of you. These include scrapping bonus payments for our staff, reducing their purchasing authority to £50, cancelling all training and other non-revenue generating activities and rationalising our management structure. These should ensure we make our increased targets for the coming year, keep our share price up and keep everyone happy."

Douglas smiled as he considered who the chairperson included in his 'everyone', and noted that 'rationalising our management structure' was a euphemism for sacking as many managers as possible.

"So this is the chamber of organisational wounds?"

Sam nodded in the affirmative in response to Douglas's question.

"So each of these represent a type of 'wound' which organisations may suffer or have suffered?"

Sam nodded again.

"These are symptoms of some of the things which get in the way of organisations fulfilling their true business potential, and, being productive places in which people can work."

"This first one looks like 'Greed and Short Termism' to me."

"Spot on Douglas, accumulation for its own sake and for the benefit of the few."

Douglas recalled the television programme 'Mind of a Millionaire' where similar characteristics were demonstrated.

"I think you will see that this combined wound – greed and short termism is at the core of all other wounds. Most major businesses operate through these two principles – to create as much return on investment as possible to benefit a small number of people in as short a time span as possible. The City orchestrates the process by penalising businesses that don't perform as expected. This sucks the passion out of many businesses, where making money becomes more important than delivering the service the business was set up for in the first place."

Douglas remembered that he had read about this in a book by Arie de Geus * where he had identified two types of organisations – the Economic Organisation, who's prime aim was to make money, and the second the Organic Organisation who continued to operate with values and vision. His research had shown that the latter survives far beyond the life span of the Economic Organisation.

As they left this first experience behind, they entered another section of this vast chamber that seemed to stretch out into infinity. Sam, with his hand on Douglas' elbow, gently guided him to his left and on to a path leading through large wooden gates and into a huge works yard. There were massive piles of metal all at different stages of processing, creating an almost lunar type landscape. As they walked on, they could see rows and rows of men with shovels shifting, what Sam told Douglas, was pig iron.

---

*'The Living Company' Arie de Geus

"That rings a bell?" Douglas turned to Sam". Is this the famous, or perhaps infamous, pig iron handlers which Freddie Taylor* told us about?"

"Yes indeed. This is where 'Scientific Management' began. Where Mr Taylor worked out how much pig iron each man should shovel, and how much he should be paid."

"They were paid by the amount they shovelled rather than the time they worked. And this led on to the concept of piece work, which is still used in some shape or form in the twenty first century."

"These guys certainly earned their money." Douglas was amazed at how hard the men were working, in very hot temperatures and in a dusty, smelly environment.

"Let's move on." Sam pointed the way. They left this massive industrial plant and walked together through a light mist, on to another industrial site. The experience, Douglas thought, reminded him of his weird and wonderful 'journeys' he had with Lise.

Douglas could recognise the next set of buildings they were approaching, mainly because he had seen them in their run-down form in various parts of the United Kingdom.

"Textile Mills?" he asked Sam.

"Yes, once, I believe, part of your country's industrial landscape. Let's go inside for a quick look."

They walked in through the main gates and into the factory itself.

"Amazing." Douglas thought. "We just walked straight into a major factory without any form of security. Changed days indeed!"

As they stepped into the factory itself they were hit by the deafening sound of the mechanical looms

---

*Considered to be the father of Scientific Management

and other machinery, and the dust filled atmosphere.

"At least we have better working conditions these days." Douglas turned to Sam who had a wry smile on his brown leathery face.

"Just hold that one for a while," he replied, "until we get to our next destination."

"A lot of the workers are just kids, they should be in school rather than in a factory." Douglas exclaimed rather indignantly. "And the rest mostly women. Cheap labour I suppose!"

"Still a key factor in major companies profits." Sam replied.

Douglas found the atmosphere quite repugnant.

"I don't know how they managed to survive working in these conditions. It's no wonder life expectancy was so low then." He turned to Sam and said, "Can we move on? What's next?"

"Let's move quickly to a present day scene so that you can compare the conditions."

Again, as they walked out of the factory gates they passed through a light mist, which eventually opened out on to a massive factory complex, surrounded by a large wire fence with barbed wire on top.

Douglas hadn't taken long to notice the change in temperature – the sun was scorching down on them – and the obvious change of country.

"The Far East?" Douglas quizzed Sam.

"Yes" Sam responded. "Shall we go in?"

This time there was massive security.

"A sign of the times." thought Douglas. However, Sam and he were able to walk straight through without being stopped. Douglas was about to ask Sam why this had been possible when he remembered his experiences with Lise when they both became invisible.

"Let's just go with the flow." he had thought. The buildings here were only double storeys compared with the massive factories they had experienced previously. The size of the whole complex though was two to three times as big as that in the United Kingdom.

As they walked in, Douglas was almost overcome with the heat and the atmosphere of the place.

"This is like a hell hole!"

Sam nodded in agreement. "What was it you said about better working conditions these days?"

As far as he could see, there were rows and rows of machines with people cutting and sewing items of clothing creating a constant cacophony of sound which Douglas found almost unbearable.

"And, the vast majority are young kids. Most can't be more than eleven or twelve."

"And some quite a bit younger." Sam added.

"So what are they producing, and for whom?"

"This is a sports wear manufacturer, making designer sportswear for the European and United States market."

"Where they will no doubt sell for exorbitant prices?"

"Indeed". Sam shook his head. "Have a walk round and have a look."

Douglas had remembered reading in the magazine 'Resurgence' that to pay the golfer Tiger Woods for one day's endorsement, Nike spends as much as the daily wages of 14,000 Thailand Nike sub-contract workers.

Douglas didn't really want to spend too much time there, but felt obliged to have a closer look. He was quite appalled at what he saw and amazed that there was nothing really being done to address these injustices.

"Low pay, high profit margins?" Douglas turned to Sam with a feeling of profound sadness combined with anger welling up inside.

"Same as before!" Sam replied, and again beginning to usher Douglas towards the door and on to the next venue.

"Only one more to see in relation to this particular wound."

Douglas was relieved to hear it! They walked slowly and silently together out of the complex and on to their next stop and to the next emerging scene.

A dusty road lined with a variety of half built houses, people, vehicles and animals seemingly milling everywhere. Horns blasting, people shouting, beggars sitting by the roadside hoping for some meagre contribution and the smell of untreated sewage. "India?" Douglas stopped and turned to Sam.

"Right again!"

"I've been before. We investigated the possibility of relocating our call centre at 'Guardian Angel' out here. In the end, we decided against it. Although, since moving, I believe their call centres have been integrated with those of Universal Bank who moved here four years ago."

"Let's have a look at one example of those call centres." Sam was dodging his way through the throngs of people and animals.

"Here we are."

It was an unprepossessing complex, purpose built by the look of it. A modern lego type building which no doubt cost the minimum to build. They again breezed past security un-noticed and into the building. It seemed to Douglas to be almost identical to the scene in the Far East, except the rows and rows of people were sitting at desks in front of their computer screens, each with their phone set in place, and thankfully there appeared to be no child labour involved.

"The noise is deafening." Douglas had to shout to make himself heard above the din.

"Just as well they can't hear it with their headsets on." Sam shouted back.

"Can we go outside?" Douglas also found this place oppressive.

"Fancy working there?" Sam smiled "I wonder how long the Directors of the business would last working in a place like that!"

"They wouldn't!" Douglas replied, rather louder than he needed to as they were now outside.

"And I know for a fact that the labour costs here are around a quarter of what businesses have to pay in the UK. There's a definite pattern in all these scenarios Sam. Low pay, high profits. Not too difficult to work out that the 'Wound' being demonstrated here is Exploitation?"

"Correct again – a bit like 'exploitation through the ages,' from Freddie Taylor to modern call centres and processing centres. Good title for a book?" Sam chuckled this time.

"Not that this is funny," Sam came back to Douglas, "Not funny at all!"

As he walked away from the scene Douglas breathed a sigh of relief, not simply because of what he had experienced but because he had managed to extricate himself from the thinking which had helped to create that level of exploitation.

Unfortunately, Douglas thought, this type of approach was not confined to the industries they had observed. Low pay was the norm rather than the exception. Exploitation took on a number of guises. One he had come across recently was a major drinks retailer who authorised single manning of shops even if they were located in areas where armed robberies were commonplace. Double manning which is the safe option, was frowned on as it upset their wage cost ratio. The hospitality/ hotel business and general retailers came into the same category, keeping both wage levels and manning levels down to ensure maximum profits. It was also reported that some hotel groups in London had taken exploitation to new levels – this time of customers – when they increased room rates on the evening of the July 2005 bombings to take advantage of people stranded in the capital overnight. On this occasion their Machiavellian approach was publicly exposed.

Douglas would love to take the Directors and senior managers of some businesses responsible for the exploitation he had seen and simply ask "Why?" Could there be a way of wakening these people up from this process of greed and exploitation, to actually realise that we are all in this together. Sadly, as he had observed in his own business, it was difficult to get many people to take a 'Big Picture' view of things.

Sam nudged Douglas in the side and pointed ahead at the next emerging scene. Douglas had been deep in thought and hadn't even noticed that they had arrived for yet another exposure. This scene appeared at first to be much less dramatic than the previous few. It was again a big open plan space filled with people sitting at desks working almost silently at their computers. Desks were set out in small groupings of four, and Douglas reckoned that there must have been around a hundred or so of these units. The energy levels within the office were so low, Douglas began to think he was watching the living dead! Occasionally, someone would get up and walk lifelessly to someone at another work space and have a brief conversation before walking slowly back to their own desk. It was as if they had given up and were going through the motions of living.

At the end of the office there was a glass panelled meeting room where about ten people were sitting around a boardroom table. Douglas and Sam slipped in at the back and listened to the proceedings.

The Chairperson of the group was sitting at the top of the table and had been explaining how they were intending to restructure the department and introduce some new IT systems over the next three months. The other participants sat around the table displaying a variety of disinterested and de-energised body language. Two had their head in both hands and looked as if they had let go, their heads would drop on to the table. A number were slouched in their chairs, some with arms folded and a couple with their hands cupped behind their heads. What they all shared was a look of resignation about, and disengagement from, the information that was being imparted. And most of the time they made no eye contact with the Chairperson.

"So that's what we plan to do." The Chairperson was bringing the meeting to a close. "I know it's a large number of major changes which have to be implemented over a short time period, and I'm sure you will all be up for it."

"You must be joking," thought Douglas. "These guys look as if they'd given up the ghost a long time ago!"

"So what do you think?" he continued. Complete

silence. Not one response, although one person looked up and made eye contact with him before checking the time on his watch.

"No comments, thoughts, ideas on what I've presented?"

Mostly silence except for some rumblings of frustration from those wanting to get away.

"OK, don't say you didn't have the chance to contribute. Meeting over."

The participants managed to stir themselves sufficiently to stand up and walk dejectedly from the room.

"Didn't even get a biscuit with the coffee." Douglas overheard one of them say. "And the coffee was awful!"

Douglas smiled and shook his head as he turned to Sam.

"Looks like they've given up – allowed themselves to be disempowered."

"Is this the next 'wound,' disempowerment?"

"Yes, together with 'hopelessness,' where no one is willing to challenge anyone or anything."

"There is fear there also?" Douglas asked

"Yes of course. Disempowerment arises out of fear, as does hopelessness. The next chamber will show you more overt fear based behaviours where fear is used as an away-from motivator."

"I'm not sure what that means."

"Some one who is motivated in this way takes action in order to move away from the consequences of not doing. Like only getting out of bed in the morning because you are afraid of being late for work, or producing a great performance in sport because you are afraid of losing the game."

"That can work though, can't it?"

"Yes it can. Fear can be a short-term motivator, but consider the consequences of the continuous stress it creates. And, you have to keep increasing the deterrent to keep it working."

Douglas could hear one manager tell his staff (as he referred to them), that unless they got their act together they'd be out of a job.

"In other words, if in doubt, frighten them?"

"I'm afraid so Douglas. As fear is perpetrated in society, so it is used as a means of control in the workplace. As if there wasn't enough terror in our world, we still seem to think it's okay to terrorise or frighten people in organisations."

Douglas nodded his agreement as they moved on to the next section.

There was a whole series of scenarios in the next section that covered a considerable area of the arena. In fact it appeared to Douglas that the arena changed its size and shape depending on the particular set of scenarios. Douglas strolled through the various areas with an air of déjà vu. There was a very smart dining area populated by a few Armani-suited individuals being served by a brigade of attentive black and white clad waiters. There was a reserved car park separate from the main car park filled with top of the range executive models as well as some snazzy sports models. Douglas chuckled when he saw the private lift adjoining the car park. Memories of 'Guardian Angel.'

Sumptuous offices with great views and lavishly appointed boardrooms completed the overall scene. The incumbents all looked very pleased with themselves.

"And so they should." a part of Douglas couldn't help thinking. Yet, he was pretty sure he knew what this represented. He had indulged in it himself at 'Guardian Angel'.

"Self Importance?"

"Correct again Douglas. Self Importance together with 'Ego'."

Douglas recalled his terrifying coach journey with his ego in charge, and smiled to himself at the thought.

"It seems a bit as if being successful is unacceptable." Douglas was uncomfortable with some of the implications of what he observed.

"Ah! I can understand your concerns," Sam put his arm around Douglas's shoulder again. "There is nothing implicitly wrong with success. Far from it. It's more complex than that, as you know from your recent exercise with your own team."

"How did he know about that?" was Douglas's immediate reaction, before dismissing the thought, as nothing really surprised him by now.

"It's how people interpret true success, and how they handle it that really matters."

Douglas nodded in agreement. It's what he had wakened up to at 'Guardian Angel.' A solitary indicator shouldn't measure success. He had seen that when people truly subscribed to the company vision and trusted that the business would be managed through its core values, success was something that touched every one.

"As you know, your society reveres the great wealthy ones." Sam laughed as he pretended to bow down as if paying homage to these idols of modern society. "As if to accumulate wealth was the real purpose of life. This doesn't mean people shouldn't enjoy their wealth; its how they create it and what they do with it. Yes?"

"Enron, amongst others that come to mind, is the worst example of those that have been exposed."

"There had also been a considerable backlash in the UK against what are referred to in the media as 'fat cats,' Douglas explained, with inflated salaries, huge bonuses and extremely generous pension entitlements, and possibly most amazing of all, being awarded these when their companies were underperforming or collapsing. On top of which, many underperformers had also been awarded quite obscene pay-offs to leave the business."

"If people can relinquish their self importance and avoid being driven by their ego we would be on the right lines."

Yes indeed, a sentiment, which struck home, Douglas thought, as he remembered his reserved parking space and special lift to the seventh floor at 'Guardian Angel'. One of his first acts at 'Silver Waters' will be to scrap reserved car-parking spaces.

As they walked on further, the height of the roof seemed to suddenly lower and Douglas became conscious of a great rumbling sound like distant thunder. As the noise increased in volume, Douglas realised they were now standing in an underground train station that, from its general condition, looked as if it belonged in London. The train emerged from the darkness of the tunnel, brakes screeching intermittently as the driver brought the train to a halt. As the doors opened a heaving mass of humanity emerged from the train. As they flooded out disregarding anyone in their way, faces fixed with well-practiced looks of resignation, the train seemed to fill up again and again. It was an endless stream of unenthused human beings.

"Rush hour in London?" Douglas asked.

"Yes it is, although it could also be many other cities."

"They look so disconnected, simply going through the motions of living. They're like the living dead, on their way to another day in purgatory."

"That's unfortunately what work means to many people in our society."

"Hey! Jump on and listen in." Sam had swung round in the opposite direction and pushed Douglas into an open train that appeared behind them. This was an overland train which was filling up with the same tired looking people as those he had observed coming out of the tube.

They sat down opposite four people, two men and two women, who were seated opposite each other with a table between.

"Just listen," Sam whispered to Douglas.

"Thank God it's Friday again!"

"Too right, another bloody week over with and only two more and I'm off on holiday. Can't wait."

"I'm dying for a holiday right now."

Each person was making their own contribution.

Sam leaned forward and tapped Douglas on the forearm "I hope she doesn't." he whispered with an impish grin on his face, which reminded him very much of Lise.

"She doesn't what?" Douglas replied.

"Doesn't die for a holiday." Sam gave Douglas a quizzical look as if to say, "You can see what I mean?"

Then he stood up and signalled to Douglas that they were leaving the train. As they stepped off, the guard blew his whistle, the doors shut and the train moved out of the station and dissolved into the distance leaving them standing back in the arena again.

"All a bit depressing Sam. Have you got anything a bit more uplifting to see?"

"Yes, of course. All in good time though. This gives us some idea of what we have to contend with, and yet we have only just scratched the surface. We haven't even looked at how commercial companies have become slaves to the City or non-profit making organisations have become slaves to management dogma. The final scenario can be seen as an outcome of many of the other wounds. Disconnection and Resignation, part of the legacy of organisational evolution, and we will have time, if you stay with me, to explore ways of reversing this decline." Sam looked at Douglas with eyebrows raised.

"Of course I'll stay with you. Why wouldn't I?" Sam gave Douglas a knowing look he had seen many times before.

"I think we've probably seen enough 'Wounds' for the moment. Let's move on."

Sam picked up the pace and led Douglas toward an exit. They walked together along an enclosed pathway that emerged into a dimly lit room about the size of a large boardroom. The floor was covered in a well-worn carpet which looked as if it had been predominately red in earlier times. The room had a musty smell about it as if it lacked ventilation, which of course it did. Along each side were old cabinets, some with glass doors, some solid oak and in the middle a large solid oak table that, like all the other pieces of furniture, looked as if it had been around for many, many years.

Strewn across the table were parchment documents that looked to Douglas like old contracts.

"The Chamber of Contracts or Agreements." Sam announced almost at the same moment as Douglas had the thought.

"This is where we may find the source of the consensus contracts which most people live by in organisations."

"You're losing me now." Douglas was still reeling a bit from the 'Chamber of Wounds.'

"I think you are familiar with the concept of consensus reality?"

Douglas nodded in agreement. Consensus reality, he understood, was the outcome of an individual's personal contract.

"You will be familiar with this concept once I provide some examples. Let me go back one stage."

"A personal contract is an agreement that we make with ourselves early in our lives about ourselves, about other people, about the world, about life etc. This contract will continue to inform our reality and our behaviour unless we can awaken from our deep sleep. We can have contracts across many areas of our lives and they will encompass our 'beliefs' and 'rules' filters which I believe you know about?" Douglas nodded.

"We might, for example, have a contract which says I cannot establish successful long term relationships. Can you guess the consequences of this type of contract?"

"A series of unsuccessful relationships?" Douglas suggested.

"Consensus contracts are agreements which have been established on a wider scale including more than one person. These can be evident on a global and an organisational level."

"A good example of an old global contract was the belief that the world was flat. When Galileo claimed it was round, he was, of course, ridiculed because the consensus contract said the earth was flat. So too in organisations, and also within certain sectors of business, people will tell you that this is the 'way it is,' much like the flat earth society believes in their own myth. True contracts are passed on from one cohort of workers to the next just like the oral traditions of indigenous peoples."

Sam walked across to the table and beckoned Douglas to join him. They both leaned on the table to view the documents that were lying out on the table.

"Just something I prepared earlier." Sam's laughter lifted Douglas's spirit.

"Look, these are the ones we will examine before you get the chance to rewrite them."

Douglas checked the title of each. He recognised them from his own experience of organisations.

'Them and Us'
'Trust No One'
'Look After Number One'
'Not Invented Here'
'Blame, Blame, Blame'
'If in Doubt, use Fear'

Douglas braced himself to read the brief statements which accompanied each heading. He picked up the first 'Them and Us' and took a deep breath.

"Go on Douglas, read it to me." Sam hoisted himself up onto the table with some difficulty, attempting, Douglas thought to lighten the atmosphere and Douglas's mood which had been gradually worsening over the journey.

"This is a nightmare!" Douglas exclaimed picking up the contract.

"Oh dear Douglas. Watch your language or you'll soon be heading for one!" Sam leaned forward shaking his index finger in mock parental style.

"Heading for… ?" Douglas caught himself short of adding 'what' as he realised what Sam was getting at. "Feels as if I'm already there…"

"I think not." Sam said quietly, waiting for Douglas to begin reading out the 'Them and Us' contract.

He cleared his throat and began…

'Them and Us.'

"In organisations there will always be a 'Them' and an 'Us'. The 'Them' will always refer to managers (at any level) and the 'Us' to those who report to managers. In some cases you can be both part of a 'Them' and also be part of an 'Us'. This will be the case for middle managers in particular.

"Being a part of 'Us' you have to develop a cynicism towards 'Them', and be sceptical about any changes 'They' propose, no matter if 'They' are productive or unproductive. 'Them' can never be part of 'Us' because once you become part of 'Them' you give up your right to be a member of 'Us'. This will ensure that we can never come truly together, to trust each other or to achieve our true potential."

Douglas recognised only too well what this contract says.

"Hasn't there always been a 'Them' and 'Us'?" Douglas said looking up at Sam's weather beaten face. "From ancient time there have been officers in the army, foremen looking after the slaves, religious leaders?"

"Not necessarily the best models on which to build the organisations of the future?"

"Granted, and isn't this just part of human nature to behave like this?"

"And so we're back to consensus reality and

consensus contracts." Sam jumped down from the table and stood in front of Douglas. Douglas was not a tall man yet if he stood his full height he was able to look straight over the top of Sam's head.

"Where are you going with that Sam?" Douglas bent his head down so that he could make eye contact with Sam. As he looked directly into his eyes it was as if each one contained the entire universe, such was the depth of connection.

"Because people believe that these behaviours are part of human nature, they also accept there is nothing they can do about it, and follow the masses that all think in this way. Think of it as accepted common practice rather than human nature. Can you recognise the difference this makes?"

"It makes it possible to change if it's the former." Douglas nodded his head in recognition of the fact and agreement with Sam.

"And you're the man to make that change happen!" Sam slapped Douglas on the back as he laughed heartily once more.

He is amazing thought Douglas. Amidst this potential doom and gloom he is able to find humour and lighten the load they were carrying.

"Once we've viewed all the contracts, you can start the process of change." Sam lifted the next contract and gave it to Douglas.

'Trust no One.'

"When you trust someone you leave yourself open to have that trust abused. People will use your trust to take advantage of you, or to let you down by not repaying your trust with commitment. When it comes down to it, its always better not to take the risk to delegate work out. This will lead to break downs in the organisation, mistakes, unnecessary expenditure and sometimes to business

failure. It is therefore logical to remain safe and trust no one."

As Douglas read this contract he could again feel that uncomfortable reaction in the pit of his stomach that was reminding him that there had been – and perhaps still was – something of this agreement evident in his own behaviour as a Chief Executive. He could see how limiting this was in allowing people to contribute fully to business success and yet he knew that he indeed had been let down in the past.

"This is a kind of 'covering your backside' contract." Douglas turned to Sam smiling. Sam gave him one of his quizzical looks in return.

"It's similar to 'if in doubt, do it yourself,' which is a result of not being prepared to trust people to get on with the job themselves. What this, in effect, does is to limit the development and ultimate potential of your people. Without opportunities to make mistakes and learn, people will stagnate as you have already seen in the Chamber of Wounds."

Douglas recalled the memories of all the reports he had 'corrected' at best, and, at worst, completely rewritten. This contract also leads to the vast quantity of forms which organisations produce to record all sorts of information thought Douglas.

"Lack of trust is also one of the factors which destroys the effectiveness of teams." Sam added.

"Could be a contributing factor in sustaining the 'Them and Us' contract." Douglas had started to think out loud.

"They will all be interrelated in some way or other." Sam responded whilst preparing the next document for Douglas to read.

'Look after Number One.'

"Avoid any real co-operation with anyone outside the

business unless it provides business benefit to ourselves. This includes competitors, suppliers, business partners and the community. It is better in fact to hate your competitors; to see them as a threat to your business. Only co-operate if it leads you to gaining a competitive advantage over them.

"Suppliers should, where possible, be screwed into the ground on costs and should not be taken into consideration during any cost cutting programme that we may introduce. If we have to, we will dump them to provide cost benefits. This relates also to any business partnerships in which we may be involved.

"And, finally, the community's welfare should only be considered if it leads to good PR and ultimately to increased market share and profits."

"Mm." Douglas was once again in contemplative mood as he recalled the times when he had expressed similar sentiments, particularly in relation to competitors. "It's a bit on the harsh side but there has to be some truth in that surely?" He said turning to Sam.

"Where do you see the truth?" Sam always seemed to be really enjoying the process. Even when challenging Douglas he seemed to be able to do it in a subtle way. There was no aggression in his manner, just a desire to explore an issue together.

"Well, you do need to be better than your competitors – have that differentiating factor which attracts more people to your business than your competitors?"

"Fair point, and would you say there would never be any benefit in co-operating with your competitors?"

"I'm sure that there could be some instances within some sectors of business where there could be benefits in co-operating."

"You see Douglas, as long as we all subscribe to a consensus reality, then it becomes our reality and we have difficulty in seeing beyond it."

"I've experienced this so many times over the past months, I should be used to it by now. I can go part of the way with this at the moment. Accepting that the aggressive approach is counter productive to ourselves and our society as a whole, whilst still believing that while we operate within the current conditions then we have to be able to compete."

"And, I'd be willing to concede almost totally on the relationships with suppliers, partners and the community. It's strange how some businesses see suppliers as almost 'the enemy' – a necessary evil, rather than someone to work closely with for our mutual benefit. And more and more I have become aware of the contribution (productive and unproductive) that we can make to our communities."

"A good point at which to move on. You will get the chance to rewrite these later, so you can make your own adaptations which suit where you are right now." Douglas smiled as Sam passed him the next contract.

'Not Invented Here!'

"New ideas are generated by senior managers only, preferably from the most senior. When presented with an idea from someone outside senior management or outside the company, we can feign interest but will not act upon it immediately. This allows us to retain the responsibility for any future successes of the business as well, of course, as gaining from them."

Douglas laughed quietly to himself when he finished reading.

"Yes, I have experienced this also," Douglas

admitted, "both as a young manager and eventually as Chief Executive. I don't think it was always a conscious act, probably more based on the perception of the person presenting the idea."

"You do agree this exists in organisations?"

"Oh definitely. I've observed it also in non-profit making organisations where there is a high level of intellectual snobbery. Academia is a good example of this, as is the medical profession. I remember reading about a young Australian doctor, Bill Marshall, who suggested to his professors that stomach ulcers could be caused by bacterium known as Helicobacter Pylori, and was met with the response, 'No way. That can't be true.' We all know ulcers are caused by stress." (A consensus reality of the time)

"He has, of course been proven correct and his suggested treatment is now used extensively and successfully throughout the medical profession."

"A great example of consensus reality blinding us to an amazing discovery and an indication of the potential that organisations have available to them and seldom use."

Douglas nodded, making a mental note to remember his stomach ulcer tale back at 'Silver Waters.'

"And so to the final two for this visit." Sam grimaced slightly, "These are probably two of the most destructive contracts in use today."

He handed Douglas the first of the two documents he was holding.

'Blame, Blame, Blame!'

"When things go wrong, we must always find someone, or some people to blame. If we are not included amongst those who are blamed, we must ensure people know this, otherwise we will be tainted by their mistakes. A good

tactic here is to distance oneself from the person or persons involved, – to disconnect from them. If people make errors then they should suffer the consequences. Also, when things go wrong within our own area of work, we must always seek someone to blame outwith our area, thus sustaining an illusion that we do not make mistakes, or if we do, someone else caused us to make these mistakes.

"Mistakes or unfulfilled goals should also play a major part of any management meeting or review. We must always spend time examining our mistakes in detail so that we can avoid them in the future."

Douglas took a deep breath and shook his head.

"The 'Blame Culture' as we call it, is still unfortunately very prevalent within our organisations, including sport interestingly enough. I have often heard coaches being interviewed and indicating that they would be making sure the players knew exactly the mistakes they made."

"So that they can repeat them, reinforcement being one of the key principles of learning." Sam laughed heartily again.

Douglas couldn't stop himself from joining in, again amazed at how Sam could find humour even within the most difficult issues.

"I have begun to think that it's something to do with managers justifying their role. That it's easier to point out mistakes than to build on what's going well. The constant focus on mistakes drains the energy from individuals and teams. Building on what's gone well, creates the energy to deal better with the mistakes."

"Hey! Lise has done a good job on you!"

"Our whole society seems obsessed with blame – we see it in the papers, on TV and particularly with politicians who have developed it into a fine art.

'Thou shalt not take responsibility' seems to be a rule that has become what you call consensus reality."

"This sadly has been the case for some time, so you'd better get moving and start reversing the trend."

"We had started the process at 'Guardian Angel.' We had begun to stop the reflex action of disconnecting and dissociating when something went wrong in some part of the business. We were developing the ethos of Support and Community."

"Support and Community? A great concept." Sam nodded his head in approval, his white teeth shining brightly against his dark brown skin each time he smiled.

"I want to make this a key part of our culture at 'Silver Waters'. I want to drag people out of this mire of blame and into a new way of perceiving success and failure. Into the idea of everyone being part of 'Us' and conveying 'Them' to the waste disposal unit!"

"Good job!" Sam put his arm round Douglas's shoulder and gave him a squeeze.

"Thanks!" Douglas had lost any feeling of inhibition now and enjoyed the support he was getting from Sam.

"And," Sam broke off and handed the second document to Douglas "This is the last contract we will look at right now. We have limited time, and these looked to be the most important."

'If in doubt, use Fear!'

"This is the ultimate motivator. It not only motivates, it also controls. It is never a good idea to relinquish too much control. If you believe this is happening then introduce some element of fear. The most common and easily used tactics include threatening loss of employment, loss of job

status, removal of bonuses, restructuring of the business and potential closure of the business. These are all excellent and easily implemented ways of controlling and motivating. Use language which implies fear, for example 'heads will role,' 'cuts will be inevitable,' 'it's a cut throat business,' 'some of you will not survive the latest downturn,' 'if you can't cut it then you won't survive,' 'it's a disaster waiting to happen.'

"When there is a downturn in the economy, then quickly resort to fear tactics to keep your workforce on their toes. If there is no downturn evident, then look for ways to create the possibility of one."

Douglas stood quietly looking at the ground and slowly shaking his head.

"I can hear myself say some of this stuff – it's what everyone expects when things are tough in business. It's like consensus behaviour, as if we have to go down that route!"

"Consensus behaviour stemming from consensus reality?"

"Yes Sam, I suppose that's true. I'm just at a loss right now, having seen and heard all this stuff we've been looking at. It's almost overwhelming, so powerful that reversing it can seem impossible."

"A huge challenge it is, impossible it is not." Sam could sense that Douglas was flagging and in need of a change of focus.

"Immediately you leave here you must write down what you have seen and what you have read. You must then rewrite these contracts as a basis for your real work in creating a new model for a business's organisational life. I'm sure Lise will be delighted to help you." Sam's smile split his face again as he slapped Douglas in the middle of his back.

"You mean I have to leave now?" Douglas actually looked a bit disappointed that this fascinating journey was soon to be over.

"For the time being my good friend. We may have more to do in the future. Come I'll show you the way out."

They walked slowly and carefully back to the point at which they had met.

"I haven't really found out anything about you Sam. Where you come from, why you are here to guide me on this amazing experience and what you do when you're not doing this?" These were only a fraction of the questions Douglas wanted to ask and yet didn't seem to have the presence of mind to remember any of the others.

"None of that is really important for you to know except perhaps that I am a descendant of the Inca people of Peru. The important thing for you is to ensure you remember this experience and to remember to write down your recollections. Goodbye my dear friend."

Sam stepped towards Douglas and hugged him. Douglas, much less inhibited than before hugged him back.

"Go well!' Sam turned and walked slowly away into the depths of the cavern.

Douglas made his way gingerly back towards the entrance, back to that door. Will it be open he wondered. As he approached the gateway he could see light streaming into the cave. So bright it was that he had to close his eyes as he stepped through onto the other side.

Chapter Nine

New Contracts

"For if a man should dream
of heaven and,
waking, find
within his hand a flower
as a token that he
had really been there ....
What then,
What then?"

Thomas Wolfe

Douglas rubbed his eyes to ease the effects of the bright sunlight and found himself lying in bed looking out of his bedroom window.

"What a fantastic sunrise." Douglas's wife, Pat, had wakened almost at the same time as he had.

"Absolutely brilliant."

"You been dreaming again?"

Douglas was still half asleep, still not sure what world he was inhabiting.

"It was so real, so very real."

"And interesting?"

"More than interesting. Mind-boggling might be a better phrase. But I must now make some notes."

Douglas had just remembered Sam's parting words and shot out of bed, grabbed a notebook and pen from a small table at the window and headed out of the room.

"Sorry, need to do this immediately." Douglas shouted back to Pat as he half ran, half toppled down the stairs towards his study. Douglas sat for over an hour writing down everything he could remember about his dream. This wasn't as difficult as he had found in the past. He was amazed at his level of recall and how lucid his dream had been. It still felt real to him as if he had actually experienced the cavern and the events with Sam. They reminded him of some of the experiences he had had with Lise.

* * *

"It was so real!"

"So I gather." said Lise "I think that could be about the tenth time you've told me."

They were sitting in Douglas's office at 'Silver Waters.' Douglas had taken Lise through his journey, step by step and had even rewritten the 'contracts' out as best he could. They were obviously not absolutely accurate reproductions and yet Douglas was pleased that they conveyed the key elements of the documents.

"And," Douglas looked very smug, "I have also rewritten each of the 'contracts,' so that I now have the beginnings of our new consensus contracts on which we can build the business for the future."

"Great news! Are you going to share these with me?"

"There are six in all. I've indicated what the original contract was and how I've re-named them before reading them to you."

Douglas moved a neat pile of papers from the side of his desk in front of him and picked up the first sheet.

"'Them and Us' becomes 'US.Com'." Douglas began reading the contents of his new 'contract.'

'US.COM'

"At the source of successful teams are people who are willing to take responsibility for their contribution to the outcomes of the team. They accept that their life is their business, and that they are therefore all running their own business. We call this business I.com."

Douglas broke off for a moment.

"This was my development from the work we did together at Guardian Angel around empowerment and the need for people to take personal responsibility for their outcomes. Remember?"

Lise nodded and smiled, conveying a sense of satisfaction at Douglas's transformation.

"Anyway, back to the contract."

"For organisations to operate consistently effectively over time each I.com (or individual) becomes part of 'US.COM.' People understand and take responsibility for their contribution to 'US.COM.' In an 'US.COM' business there is no 'Them', only 'US'."

'US.COM' can then build strong relationships with customers, suppliers, business partners, competitors and the wider community, hence we have ..."

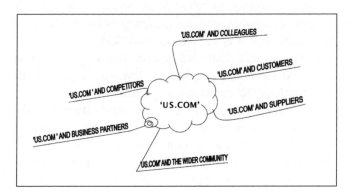

"Like it?" Douglas had that self-satisfied look that Lise knew so well by now.

"It's fabulous, a great concept."

"Not for much longer!"

"In what way?" Lise was intrigued.

"What I mean is that it won't be a concept much longer, since we will be implementing this in the business in the near future. We're working on some ideas just now."

"Any clues?"

"Not right now. Definitely later. Just now I want to share all the contracts with you."

"Great!" Lise could see what a powerful effect his dream had had on him. Well done Sam, she thought.

"Next up is 'Trust No One' which has been changed to 'Build Trust and Support'."

'Build Trust and Support'

"Trust is the foundation on which our people can grow. Trust opens the door for people to expand and grow, gives them the confidence to contribute their potential within the business. Trust's essential ally is 'Support.' When we put 'trust' in people, we will always support them when needed, especially if their first efforts are unsuccessful.

Trust between colleagues is a key to our success. It means that each of us can focus on our own contributions, knowing that our colleagues are doing like wise. This is an essential element of a successful 'US.COM'."

"It's superb Douglas. I love the way you have worded the entire contract in 'toward' language and avoided any 'away from' references."

"I learned that from Sam and purposefully avoided saying things like, 'Trust is important, because when it's broken'...etc, you know what I mean. It's like giving an opening to those people who want to use a lapse in trust to revert back to old ways with the old ' I told you they can't be trusted.' Well, of course there will be times when people will abuse the trust shown to them, that's not an excuse to screw up the whole organisation to deal with these individuals. It's like businesses that tell all their senior managers that their jobs are on the line if they don't perform, when in-fact they mean that 5% haven't been performing. But, rather than deal with that 5% they de-motivate all their managers, and in turn their work force."

Lise burst into spontaneous applause.

"Bravo! I can see I'm becoming redundant these days."

"Not so, your energy still inspires me."

"Next up is 'Look After Number One' which changes to 'Develop US.COM networks'."

'Develop US.COM Networks' as 'Business Communities'

"By opening up to the creation and development through US.COM of 'Community' within an individual business, we can extend this to include competitors, suppliers, partners and the wider community. Specifically, building closer relationships with our competitors we can agree on basic operating standards that ensures our sector of business builds a strong reputation within the market place. By developing this over time our potential customers will feel safe and secure in buying our products and services thus extending the potential market for all players in the sector. Suppliers and business partners are key members of our extended business community and the impact our business decisions have on them, and the wider community should be taken into consideration."

"Could be viewed as rather altruistic by some of your colleagues in the business world?"

"You mean you don't like the idea?" Douglas

sounded surprised as well as defensive.

"No I'm not saying I don't like it – of course I like it. I'm simply commenting that these views will be seen to be 'off the wall' by some, and downright crazy by others."

"Strange in a way, since most people will have heard of, or perhaps used the expression that 'one bad apple will destroy the whole barrel', and would subscribe to it as a concept."

"It's always harder to do something, than agree with it in principle."

"It seems obvious to me now. For example, if I visit a town or city on holiday and receive dreadful service in my chosen hotel, it will colour my whole experience of the place itself and the service provided in its hotels. It's highly unlikely I would return to the same destination, thus damaging the potential of all hotels in the area."

"The same has happened in many respects in the financial services world, with poor advice given by unethical advisers leading to a lack of trust and confidence across the whole sector."

"Indeed." Douglas felt the impact of Lise's observation in a very personal way, "And it may take some time to rebuild customers' confidence in parts of our business."

"Especially with the high salaries the top managers receive!" Lise laughed across at Douglas.

"I'm not accepting the bait to be defensive on this occasion." Douglas was smiling broadly in response to Lise's jibe. "We are in fact constructing more widely acceptable remuneration packages within 'Silver Waters' that recognise talent and performance without being disrespectful to our customers and the community at large."

"Wow! I'm sure that will create a good deal of interest when you announce it."

"I certainly hope so!" Douglas sat back and folded his arms in mock satisfaction.

"And what's next on the agenda?" Lise asked.

"Just before we move on, I believe it is also vital that we recognise the importance of our suppliers, partners and our communities. It's time to stop seeing our businesses as isolated money making machines for top management, shareholders and the City in general."

Lise nodded in quiet agreement whilst realising the enormity of such a task.

"Right." Douglas shuffled through his notes deciding to move on.

"'Not Invented Here' becomes 'Involve and Engage all Colleagues, Customers, Partners and Suppliers'."

'Involve and Engage all Colleagues, Customers, Partners and Suppliers'"

"In order to access the potential of people who are involved in our business we will stay both open to ideas and suggestions from all parties as well as actively encouraging participation. We recognise that everyone who works in the business has potential to contribute to its ongoing development and that we will seek innovative ways of engaging their creativity for the benefit of themselves and the business by seeking contribution from outside the management team. We recognise the diversity of viewpoints which are available to us, and by operating in this way we will build stronger, more productive relationships with all concerned."

"So you include customers and suppliers as well as colleagues?" Lise probed Douglas.

"Definitely. I'm amazed at how some companies

for example, view their suppliers as the 'enemy' rather than as a working partner. And who better to ask for development ideas than the people who use your products and services. Then, of course, we also must involve all colleagues in finding new and better ways to operate. I've certainly learned the hard way that neither I nor my colleagues in management have all the answers. In fact, as you so pointedly demonstrated to me at 'Guardian Angel,' it was often me who was at the source of the reluctance to contribute."

"What ideas do you have to implement this?" Lise was taking on the logical-rational questioning route for a change.

"We started a number of initiatives at 'Guardian Angel' and were beginning to reap the benefits before the takeover. I will put these on the table here and at the same time be careful not to inhibit ideas from other quarters. Internally we worked hard to change our managers' style, encouraging them away from an ego driven/telling approach to an open coaching style where they focused on asking questions and really listening to people's contributions. A bit like you're doing just now."

"I'll take that as a compliment then?" Lise was enjoying working with Douglas again.

"Well, of course!" Douglas was also enjoying having Lise there to challenge him.

And he needed her here for this one, he thought, as he drew in a deep breath he focused on the next 'contract.'

"'Blame, Blame, Blame,' is our next challenge."

"And what a challenge!" Lise sat back in anticipation.

"I had a bit of difficulty coming up with the ideal

antithesis to this one. I toyed with replacing 'Blame' with 'Openness', and then I gave 'responsibility' a chance. In fact, I still think that would work. My final choice, for the movement though is 'Solutions, Solutions, Solutions'."

Lise pursed her lips and nodded her head in approval.

'Solutions, Solutions, Solutions'

"Our ultimate goal is to find productive solutions which will help us achieve greater success. We recognise that mistakes will be made, and that without them we will make no progress. We also recognise that mistakes can provide us with opportunities to make progress and find better ways of working.

We will encourage openness and honesty where mistakes are concerned, to create an environment where people do not cover up their mistakes or deny they ever made them.

Once we recognise we have made a mistake, we move immediately into 'Solution' mode. This applies also to long term problems which are deemed unsolvable, or are blamed on external factors which cannot be controlled."

"I've always liked the saying that 'If you're not helping to solve the problem, then you're part of it,'"

Lise really liked this one, "You know," she said, "One of my friends has been a hotel general manager in a major company for a number of years. She was telling me the other day that their annual people turnover was usually around 80%, and that was quite normal in her business. I found this absolutely amazing considering that they employ around 450 people. That's re-employing at least 360 people per year." I said to her.

"What a huge burden in terms of time and money to re-employ that number of people each year."

"I know, I said that to her."

"And what did she say?"

"She said it was a problem with their business, that most people didn't see the hotel industry, as she calls it, as a long term career. That they were poor payers, and that people had to work long unsocial hours in sometimes-difficult conditions. The strange thing is that she accepts this as the norm since she and her colleagues see it as a problem of external perception."

"So what are they doing to change that perception?"

"Nothing significantly, because they don't believe they can. They seem more comfortable continuing to blame these external factors, or other factors outside their control."

"Get that new 'Solutions' contract to her!" Douglas handed a copy to Lise.

"I know that they could change things if they chose to put their minds to it. There are solutions available if they were to look carefully."

"And what's next on the menu?" Lise again sat back with her arms folded in anticipation.

"The next is the last contract for now."

"You mean there's more to come in the future?" Lise raised her voice in mock disbelief.

"Well, you never know when I might meet up with Sam again." Douglas shrugged his shoulders, put his head to one side to mirror her body language and smiled smugly.

"'If in Doubt, Use Fear'." was the last contract Sam showed me.

"Wow! So he left the biggy to the last?"

Douglas felt that sense of being overwhelmed once again, in the same way he had during his experience with Sam.

"It's so prevalent in all aspects of our society and constantly reinforced by politicians, the media, large corporations with their own agendas to pursue, – even sports coaches will use fear as a supposed means of motivating their charges. And unfortunately a good part of the broad financial services business is built on the fear of the future, with calls to insure this or insure that, invest with us for a happy future, and so on."

"And then the companies who have looked after their investments tell them they won't get what they had promised them."

"Sadly true and something we don't want to happen at 'Silver Waters'."

"And the new contract?"

"'If in Doubt, Use Fear' becomes 'Uplift and Inspire the Spirit'."

"A wonderful change." Lise nodded her approval.

'Uplift and Inspire the Spirit…'

… "to benefit all. We recognise that fear is a very short-term motivator that causes great stress and dissociation both for individuals and organisations. We aim to create a culture that is attractive to all parties – to our current colleagues, our potential colleagues, our customers and potential customers, our suppliers, business partners and the wider community. By uplifting and inspiring people we create a productive energy which motivates people to contribute powerfully to the success of the business. Our strategies, our behaviours, our language, our organisational communication, our actions will all aim to uplift and inspire our people, providing an environment in which they can achieve self satisfaction as well as outstanding business performance."

"Our business creed will always be to UPLIFT AND INSPIRE."

As he finished Douglas took a deep breath, looked up, and a smile that started on his lips spread across his face as he turned towards Lise.

"Great stuff! And is it really possible?"

"What would stop us? Apart from ourselves perhaps, and our attachment to consensus thinking and consensus reality. The only reason that fear-based thinking and behaviour are accepted is because people have been told that's how it is. It becomes a massive consensus contract that people go along with."

"So how could this be changed within an organisation when the rest of people's experience of reality is laced with fear, and in many cases terror?"

Douglas had become conscious that a role reversal had taken place. Lise was now playing the 'unconvinced' and he was playing the teacher.

"Are you playing devil's advocate with this, or are you truly sceptical about the possibility of succeeding in changing business cultures?"

"Helping you to sharpen your sword for the battles ahead!" Lise pretended to remove a sword from its sheath and stood 'on guard' facing Douglas.

"You will be severely tested and challenged in your quest to implement these ideas. I'm posing some of the questions you will have to deal with in order to succeed with your mission. And, although you've come a long way since we first met, you will still be attached to elements of this consensus reality."

"I'm not conscious of much right now." Douglas felt a little defensiveness creeping into his response.

"You will be." Lise assured him again challenging his current perception of himself.

"In fact, I suspect it's happening to an extent right now?"

Douglas had completely forgotten that Lise could read his mind accurately, although it didn't stop him defending a bit more.

"What do you mean happening right now?"

"I think you know the answer to that?" Lise raised her eyebrows to emphasise the question.

"You will know when you have been truly challenged. You'll feel it. And when a particular change challenge causes you pain you'll know that your attachments are still with you. Do you remember when you considered scrapping the reserved parking spaces at 'Guardian Angel'?"

Douglas immediately felt his stomach and abdominal region tightening as he recalled the thought, firstly of himself giving up his space, and secondly having to tell his colleagues that this would happen. As it was, he had decided at that time that it was a step too far and had backed off.

Douglas nodded, understanding what she meant.

"Well of course I have some doubts and fears about seeing through profound change, and the challenges I will have to face. I've already indicated this to you. What I don't want to do is to express these doubts and fears by defending my own 'truth', my model of the world."

"Well said!" Lise was impressed by Douglas's ever growing capacity to understand and express these challenging issues. "Perhaps you have to focus on your own personal development before launching into a major change programme with your business?"

"I can't delay the change for long. I must let people know that we have major work to complete to create the success we desire."

"Remember 'Process and Outcome?'" Lise probed Douglas once again.

He nodded back in the affirmative.

"I know, I know, and what I'm saying is I want to keep the 'Process' moving, and I can also see that I am still attached to the 'Outcome,'"

"A sure way of feeding your own fears and doubts. You will have some fun, I'm sure, in working your way through these. Anyway, I'm off for now. I'll see you again the day after tomorrow."

As she was going out she poked her head back round the door "Why don't you check out your favourite web site again?"

Feelings of fear and uncertainty had been rising and falling within Douglas for some time now. A most uncomfortable experience – he had always been in control, certain of where he was going and what to expect. He knew from his work with Lise that 'uncomfortable' was something we have to experience in the process of change. And, the more profound the change, the greater the level of discomfort. Would he now have the mental strength, courage and most of all, energy to engineer the changes he wanted at 'Silver Waters'? From a financial perspective, Douglas was well sorted. He had invested shrewdly over the years and his package from 'Guardian Angel' had been very generous. He knew that he could land some non-executive board positions if he chose to – in fact he had already been approached by two major financial services businesses for such a position. So he knew that from a financial perspective he didn't really need to work full time.

Deep down though, he knew his work was not in opting out of this challenge; his work at 'Guardian

Angel' had been his apprenticeship he reckoned. He now needed to prepare himself, give himself time to 'heal' the wounds suffered in his departure from what he had seen was his life's work. He needed space to make sense of this bombardment of his psyche and ready himself for the challenges ahead at 'Silver Waters'.

What if, he thought, I had never met Lise, what then? Would I now be happily running 'Guardian Angel,' pleased to be part of a multi-national banking organisation? Parking in my reserved space and being whisked up to my office on the exclusive executive lift? Oblivious to the effect I was having on the results of the business. He took a deep breath and shook his head. Not a scenario he would want to contemplate. Although 'uncomfortable' on one level, he felt more connected with himself and his world than he had ever been. He knew he would accept the challenge.

He swung back round to his desk and to his laptop to access the site to which Lise had referred. These marvellous scenes from Peru which had come on top of his reading of 'The Celestine Prophesy' and particularly Fred Alan Wolf's 'The Eagle's Quest'. What had really captured his imagination was that here was an eminent theoretical physicist, author of award winning titles and residing in the rationality of left brain thinking, willing to explore the mystical and mythical world of shamanism. Not only in a theoretical sense but also through active participation. The book had also opened his thinking further around some of the understandings of perception that he had explored with Lise. He had been fascinated to learn of what is known as the 'Observer Effect' in theoretical physics, described as the sudden change in the physical property of matter... when that property is observed. Wolf had pointed out that 'what we perceive not only affects yourself, it affects the object of perception.' Both we and it are affected by the action of perception – by what we believe is out there!' As Werner Heisenberg, the founder of the uncertainty principle in quantum physics said "The path comes into existence only when you see it." This completely turns upside down the old saying that 'I'll believe it when I see it' mused Douglas, to 'I'll see it when I believe it.' A great part of the shaman's power is in their lack of inhibition in having to see the world from a left brain logical perspective. Because their beliefs were different, they perceived the world and its energies in different ways. Douglas had become more aware of this in an intuitive sense, through his amazing experiences with Lise. It had crossed his mind on a number of occasions that Lise had many of the qualities and skills of the shaman that Wolf had identified. He smiled to himself as this thought came into his consciousness once again. He wondered what further learnings he would experience through contact with the shamanic world of Peru.

These thoughts had emerged as the images from his favourite web site emerged on screen, and an overwhelming desire to be there filled his consciousness. This was definitely the place to 'sharpen his sword' for the challenges that lay ahead. Now he needed to find the means of visiting the right places and meeting the right people. He found this reasonably easily through his Internet search engine. In fact, it was only the second site he accessed. 'Healing-Journeys.co.uk' turned out to be a small bespoke business offering spiritual shamanic journeys to Peru amongst other offerings. And strangely enough their next trip fitted his schedule perfectly. All being well he would be there within the month.

Chapter Ten

Peruvian Adventure

"Only a man with a spoiled heart will go in the wrong direction."

Don Mariano

As the plane took off and banked to the left, Douglas looked down and back over Lima, and back over an unbelievable experience. He had no real idea of what to expect when he set off. Certainly, he couldn't have perceived an experience so rich and varied, so challenging and energising. He couldn't have believed the level of energy he had experienced in the various places he had visited.

Douglas closed his eyes and let his thoughts run back over the various experiences he had enjoyed – his introduction to the wonderful city of Cusco, the various ceremonies he had taken part in, and certainly nothing had prepared him for his first sight of Machu Picchu, the ancient city of the Incas. He had been amazed at how 'at home' he felt in this South American country whose culture couldn't have been much further removed from his own. He had experienced this most powerfully on his first visit to Cusco. At 11,500 feet above sea level, he had been a little apprehensive over the possibility of altitude sickness. But apart from some breathlessness, his body had coped remarkably well. Cusco or Quosquo – the native Peruvian word meaning the area of the body around the navel where our energy is centred – was so named by the Incas as the real centre of the Universe.

As he walked into the main square on that first day he had marvelled at his sense of connection. The city was an amazing mixture of Spanish architecture and Incan craftsmanship. The magnificent Catholic Cathedral had been built on top of a sacred Incan site of worship. This mirrored to some extent the way in which many Peruvians had integrated their own spiritual beliefs with those brought to them by their colonial 'masters.' Some consider this to have been a way of keeping the Spanish invaders off their backs. Douglas had spent some time wandering through the streets and markets of this beautiful city, and had purchased a number of items associated with Peruvian culture. Despite the altitude Douglas had felt a palpable connection with the place, as if the surrounding mountains were pushing their energy out towards him. He could understand why the Incas considered this to be the centre of the world.

He opened his eyes and checked the time. They had been flying for around thirty minutes as he had been recalling his first taste of what he thought of now as the real Peru.

His mind wound back as if he had pressed the fast rewind button on his video, reviewing many of the fantastic places he had visited and the ceremonies he had taken part in. He smiled to himself – or perhaps, as he thought, to his 'new self' – as he imagined what his contemporaries might think of his exploits. Or indeed what he would have thought of himself not so long ago. His experiences in Peru, allied to his learnings from Fred Alan Wolf, had sharpened his understanding even more about the challenge we have in breaking free from consensus reality – from our social and psychological conditioning. Wolf had described this by suggesting that the unconscious mind is really very conscious, always aware of what we are thinking – and is observing all the time. That, in our mind we make grooves – roadways- that we follow without thinking and that we stay in these grooves even if they give us pain and unhappiness. And, we ultimately don't notice them anymore. We accept them as our reality. He had made a note earlier to pursue the concept that Wolf had uncovered, of 'least-action pathways.' He had a sense that he could relate this to the changes he could make back in 'Silver Waters'. He felt a subtle tightening within as he thought of the potential challenges ahead.

Machu Picchu remained his most spectacular memory. He could still recall most vividly the moment this Inca marvel came into view. He had seen photographs of it many times before, and yet nothing had prepared him for the sheer grandeur of the place. This ancient city encircled by lush green and black velvety mountains. As he recalled his visit he could feel the surge of energy once more. Never before had he been so aware of the vibrational energy of natural spaces. It wasn't merely a sense of the energy. He had been able to feel it touch his own energy field. It was palpably real. It was easy to see why the Incas had built a sacred city there, and almost impossible to imagine how they had achieved it. He had gazed in wonder at the precision of the Inca craftsmen and women and compared this with current building standards in our present day 'civilised' world.

He breathed deeply into his centre – something he had learned during his travels – and recalled the ceremony in which he had participated at Machu Picchu. It had been led by the Q'uero shamans who had accompanied them to the ancient site. These shamans considered themselves to be the descendants of the Incas who had fled from their Spanish invaders and had lived at an altitude of 17,000 feet for several hundred years. They spoke only their native language of Quecha, so at ceremonies like these they were assisted by interpreters. During the ceremony the shamans called in the energy of the mountains and of the earth, pachamana – or the mother – as they call it. It had been a powerful experience which was completed by the shamans "blessing" each of the group in turn. They used their mesas for this – their ritual bundle containing sacred and powerful objects – placing it on each person's head and back. Douglas recalled the surge of healing energy he had felt as they carried out their final ritual. He had been very reluctant to leave the site, and stood in silence for some time – he wasn't sure how long – as he watched the silhouette of the city against the setting sun, almost sensing that it was returning itself to its former glory.

He jerked slightly in his seat as he felt himself beginning to fall asleep, and looked at his watch again. Something he had got out of the habit of whilst in Peru. He could sense that he was beginning to return, at least in part, to his former habitual ways. An hour gone already? He wondered whether he had been sleeping, or perhaps in a deep trance. He remembered thinking on many occasions when working with Lise whether his experiences had been real, or if he had been in a trance-induced state. He had always concluded that they had been very real, which convinced him more than ever that the world was not the three dimensional place that we are taught to believe in. He had also begun to wonder if we stored our dreams and daydreams in our unconscious minds as if they had been real events. If our unconscious minds are in constant observational mode, as Wolf suggests, then this could well be the case he thought. So we could be attached to memories that never actually took place... he laughed out loud at the possibility, and wondered what he could have installed for himself over the years.

He closed his eyes again and slipped back into his thoughts of his adventures. After Machu Picchu he had wondered if anything else would match up. In terms of scale, nothing did quite compare to the majesty of the place. And yet each other experience had its own special magic energy.

His thoughts led him through the various sacred sites he had visited and the ceremonies in which they had participated. He remembered his fascination with the Q'uero shamans. They were very typically native Peruvians and had immediately reminded him of Sam in his dream. One Shamen in particular was such an exact look-alike that he had to stop himself calling him Sam! Uncanny he thought. What struck him most was how centred, calm and in their bodies they looked. They went about their business in a straightforward, almost no-nonsense manner, yet still brought great presence to each sacred ceremony. He had loved their native dress – their ponchos, sometimes plain, sometimes patterned in bright colours and their beautifully embroidered woollen hats. Their skin was dark and weather beaten from the harsh conditions in which they lived 17,000 feet above sea level in the Andes. They were deeply connected to their life's purpose as a shaman and the powerful demands that this role placed on them within their communities. He compared their selflessness with the addiction to self-absorption that was prevalent in 'Western' society. For native Peruvians they were their healers and would be required to answer the call of their people when needed. It is not an easy role and not one they chose – rather it is chosen for them, after which they require to follow a rigorous apprenticeship to achieve the status as a shaman. The Q'uero shamans had various levels of attainment and skills, so people would choose a shaman depending on their particular strengths. Douglas recalled his one-to-one healing session with Don Mariano, one of the older and most experienced shamans. Although they couldn't converse directly – he had some help from one of the group guides – he had felt a very strong energetic connection with Don Mariano and had asked for assistance in addressing the challenges he would face back in his everyday world of work. Don Mariano had created a special offering for him, called a despacho that was made up from a variety of natural items and put together with Douglas's help. This was infused with the energy of the shaman and his connection to the natural world, and later burned during a group fire ceremony.

As he recalled this special event he wondered whether the Don's work with him would have an impact for him back in 'Silver Waters'. He took another deep breath into his centre and trusted that it would.

He recalled the water ritual they had performed at

Tipon and watching the sun set at the Temple of the Wind at Ollantaytambo. This had been particularly powerful as he remembered feeling the cooling wind on his face as he stood in a meditative state whilst the sun set slowly behind the snow capped mountains. Each place had its own special energy and connection and always there had been the sense of energetic connection with the mountains. It was as if energy was flowing down the mountainside and connecting with his own energy field. Although constantly at altitudes of between 10,000 and 12,000 feet he had felt few adverse affects, and apart from some tiredness on the first evening had felt highly energised throughout the journey. It was as if each day his energy field was being refilled with the mountain energy.

It was what he had hoped for when he had first viewed the web-cam on his PC. 'Where did all that come from?' was hardly a completed thought when Lise popped into his mind. Another coup for her he wondered.

And then there was his ayahuasca experience. He had read about this psychotropic plant in Fred Alan Wolf's book and of the author's involvement in ayahuasca ceremonies. Psychotropic plants, he was amazed to discover had been used as far back as 3000BC – archaeological findings in Ecuador had confirmed this. The meaning of the word he had discovered was 'vine of the dead'. 'Aya' in Quechua means 'spirit', 'ancestor', 'dead person' while huasca means 'vine' or 'rope'. Huascar was also, according to Incan mythology, the last Inca to die and is the guardian of the lower 'world', or Ukhu Pacha in Andean cosmology. His fascination with Wolf's tales of the plant had led him to seek out a means of experiencing its effect. Would he have been so keen if he had known what we would experience? Probably, he decided.

The ayahuasca experience hadn't been on the itinerary of Healing-Journeys, so he had had to source this part of the trip independently. He had also negotiated three days out from his guided trip and had arranged to meet up again when he came back. He had spent the day prior to the ceremony fasting, eating only a little fresh fruit and drinking water. Ayahuasca acts as a purgative, so fasting is highly recommended. Didn't stop me from being very sick, he thought. He had managed to meet up with another group of adventurers (He liked to think of himself in these terms) and book into a jungle lodge on the edge of the Madre de Dios River, a tributary of the Amazon.

He had no desire to relive the experience again in full – even in his mind. After taking the cup of thick green liquid he had lain down in the dark in a wooden hut a few hundred yards or so into the jungle and away from the compound of lodges where he was staying.

He remembered feeling fine to begin with. When the candles that were illuminating the hut were extinguished, the space took on an eerie darkness. This feeling was heightened by the permanent whistling and singing and shaking of the shamans, which coupled with the effects of the plant began to disorientate him. A buzzing and flapping at his ears – what were they? Flies, Birds? Were they real or an illusion? "Stop that singing and whistling," he had wanted to shout. "Leave me in peace to suffer."

He realised afterwards that the songs or Icaros as they are known are designed to invoke the spirits of the plants and of the dead. The icaros are used to modify and tune visions. He remembered weird visions firstly of cartoon characters who became less attractive as they came close. Doors being opened expectantly, only to find hysterical laughter when he went through them.

He opened his eyes, briefly, looked out of the window of the plane, and breathed deeply – two hours now into the flight. He went back into his thoughts still trying to make some sense of his ayahuasca experience. He had concluded previously that the experience had challenged him to face his fears head on and come through them stronger than before. It also demonstrated his courage in accepting the challenge knowing that it would be very uncomfortable. He remembered one of Lise's first lessons on change, when she emphasised that to truly change we must experience a level of discomfort. To only do what we feel comfortable doing, equates to us staying in our 'habit.' And he reckoned he had certainly taken some major steps out of his 'habit.' His experience with the butterfly had been quite magical. As a symbol of transformation it had lifted his spirits exactly when needed.

Transformation was subtle he thought, so many people are looking for the secret – one event or teaching i.e. an experience which will provide total and lasting transformation. He had begun to trust that the work he had been doing since meeting Lise, coupled with his ability to stay conscious and be consistently on his 'own case,' was having a powerful internal transformational effect.

Ayahuasca ceremonies have been used for centuries as a healing ritual. They are not used for drug induced trips in the way that western society has abused many other healing plants and substances. He was glad he had experienced the effects of the vine and felt it had opened up some previously closed internal channels.

This wasn't an experience he intended to share with his colleagues. It had been undertaken for his personal benefit, as part of his own personal growth and development. And there was much that he had seen and learned during his trip which he believed could be used to assist in bringing about the organisational change that he desired.

He sat up in his seat and took out a notebook and pen. He wanted to review the notes he had made during his journey and relate these back to his challenge at 'Silver Waters.' Douglas had learned during his first day in Peru that the most significant operative principle of behaviour within the Andean Culture was Ayni. This principle recognises the constant interchange of energy that we engage in with other humans and the natural world. For the Andeans it was like a moral code similar to the Christian teachings of "doing unto others as you would have them do unto you." It encourages them to be conscious of the type of energy they are projecting and, in everyday terms, it also meant a sharing of labour and everyday tasks. It seemed to Douglas to be beautifully devoid of ego and a great basis for a productive working culture. Too often people forget the impact their energy is having on those around them, and on the world itself, too self-absorbed to engage in this reciprocal act of sharing energy. He recalled that he had been a major culprit of this in the past. He remembered the lessons Lise had given him, particularly the impact of his behaviour and presence on those around him at 'Guardian Angel.' "Ignorance is bliss" is not a concept to which he subscribed.

Douglas smiled as he recalled the commonly used phase "There were good vibes from the meeting" or "I always have good vibes when I meet so and so." So few people he guessed would be prepared to use the full version of the word –vibration – and would be rather hesitant to suggest they had received good vibrations from someone else. And yet, as he had discovered on his travels, we do have a vibrational energy which surrounds our physical body. Whatever it was called, he had become more aware of the impact his own energy body could have on himself and on others

The Andean traditions recognise two different types of energy that can be drawn into our energy field. Sami is light refined energy – productive energy is how Lise would have described it he guessed – when we are in harmony and grounded with ourselves and the world around us. Hucha, on the other hand, is heavy or dense energy – that energy which can accumulate when we are out of balance with ourselves and our challenges or, for example, where we cannot resolve relationship issues effectively.

It seemed to Douglas that in his experience, the predominant energy in the business world was 'hucha', or the dense heavy energy. This is not what we would call 'negative' energy. It is a kind of sense of being disconnected, out of the flow – a kind of incompatible or disharmonious energy. The Andeans believe that this type of energy is exclusive only to humans.

Douglas had experimented with ways of cleaning out his 'hucha' taught to him by the Andeans. These ideas were still quite foreign to Douglas. He could understand what he was supposed to do, but his belief systems often overpowered his attempts to participate in such activities. He had realised however, the powerful effect that breathing into his "centre," or into his abdomen had on his state of mind, and general feeling of well being, and was able to work with this to his own benefit. He had also further developed his ability to place his attention on various parts of his body and direct his energy towards that part. As he considered this, he also realised that he was underestimating his capacities in this dimension as these were well beyond his experience and consciousness of only a couple of years previously.

He had also found his ability to meditate – taught to him by Lise – a great advantage during the various ceremonies in which he had participated. He had particularly enjoyed the 'open eye' meditation he had experienced at Machu Picchu. Having the opportunity to sit above the ruins looking out over the famous postcard view and beyond to the horizon, and the breathtaking skyline of the mountains. To feel their energy and sense of presence, to watch the subtle change of colour and shadow as the sun set behind them. He felt as if he was part of it all, merged with the natural energies which surrounded him. The borders between himself and his surroundings blurred, and he had a sense of internal expansion as if some channels deep within him were opening for the first time. He had never experienced this feeling of connectedness and inner growth before. It was as if his very core, his soul, had expanded within. As he recalled this amazing experience he smiled to himself with a deep sense of satisfaction and of optimism for the future.

He had been amazed, and on many occasions humbled, by the uplifting spirit and happiness of the people he had met on his travels. Most were very poor by 'western' standards and would be considered to be living in poverty; yet, they went about their daily lives with a vigour and enthusiasm for life that is seldom seen in our culture, Douglas had thought.

He had the privilege of staying with a traditional family on the island of Amantani on Lake Titticaca. Their accommodation was very basic by our standards and yet they again were happy and connected people living in a true community where ayni – or reciprocity – was part of everyday life. Just as in the communities he had read about in Guatemala, everyone in the island community assisted each other when carrying out major tasks like house building or house extensions and rather than 'fight' for the little income that tourism brought to them, they shared the business out on a rotational basis. Not really a concept he could imagine western businesses embracing!

When he had arrived in Peru, one of their guides, Julio had told them that the most important principle of Andean life and culture was Munay, or love from the heart. This was most evident in the way in which the islanders went about their daily life. Douglas, of course knew that it would be impossible to replicate the approaches to life and work which he had observed, and also recognised the hardships which these people had to endure at times, but he had allowed himself to expand his own thinking to identify ways in which he could incorporate a flavour of this into his own life and into the life of his business.

Douglas had begun to wonder whether he should give up his work and focus his energies on charitable activities, use his skills to assist those who really needed help. Or, should he stick with his current challenges and work to make a real impact in his role as Chief executive of 'Silver Waters' demonstrating to the business world that real change was possible – and effective-measured by both traditional and non-traditional means.

As he closed his eyes again he knew in his heart that he would face up to the challenges that would be presented to him in his work. His experience in Peru had strengthened his sense of purpose. He really did now have a deeply developed sense of purpose in his life, beyond his previously superficial quest for accumulation. He didn't think having material 'things' was wrong; it was just that they were not the most important element in his life. He reckoned it would be pretty well nigh impossible for anyone to visit a country like Peru, experience what he had experienced, and stay the same. Unless, of course they were content with a superficial experience, or remained 'unconscious' throughout. He wondered once again what it was that the shamans had that made them healers, and how they effected the outcomes they achieved. He himself had experienced a great sense of release as he had worked with them – released from the fear and doubt that he had been experiencing since he moved from 'Guardian Angel' to 'Silver Waters.' He felt cleansed, with renewed levels of energy and commitment to take on the big challenges that lay ahead. He felt more centred and grounded than he had ever done and knew that his newfound strength would be available when required.

He had learned that all shamans have a real connection with the vibrational force of the universe. He had come across this firstly through the work of theoretical physicist, Fred Alan Wolf, and had experienced it in person, particularly through his episode with ayahuasca. Wolf had wakened him to a simple shaman truth – that our bodies are a reflection of our thoughts! That because shamans deal with the connection between mind and body, they are able to see/sense these thoughts and where they may be affecting the body. Then, through their calling, their training and experience they were able to sense the vibrational forces within an individual. Douglas had been amazed when Don Mariano, through an interpreter, had told him that there was something else that was troubling him that he had not mentioned. And he had been right! Don Mariano was only satisfied when he had opened up to him completely.

Wolf had made sense of this in a scientific way by relating his hypothesis on a shaman's capacities to the 'observer effect' of quantum physics. "Alter the way you see reality and you alter reality." Wolf's observations and research and his first hand experience of working with shamans had opened his thinking up on ways he could effect real change back in his real world. He had heard it many times and used the phrase, "that's all very well in theory, but in the 'real world'…." He had now come to realise that what people meant was according to consensus reality, this is what we should see, think, do! His 'real' world had moved away from consensus thinking and consensus reality, but could he truly influence others to think and act differently? Could he make the impact he wanted and create a 'critical mass' of people who would assist him in creating the kind of connected organisation that he wanted?

He noted down the key elements that he could bring back in some form or other to 'Silver Waters'.

- AYNI – the spirit of reciprocity.
- COMMUNITY – built from AYNI where people genuinely work together with a sense of the 'Bigger Picture' And a practical understanding of their 'Collective Responsibility.'
- MUNAY – love from the heart and a feeling of selflessness.
- KAWSAY – our life energy that fills our universe, similar concept to 'Chi' in Eastern Traditions.
- SAMI – Refined energy and how to generate it.
- HUCHA – heavy energy and how to release it.
- POQ'PO – Our energy body – the "bubble" which surrounds us. Or morphogenic field as Wolf describes it.
- RITUAL – Creating sacred space in which to connect with healing energies. In a work sense, ensuring that meetings are set up so as to encourage the free flow of energy, ideas and knowledge amongst the group involved.

Douglas had already started this process at 'Guardian Angel' where he had been very particular in creating the type of space and atmosphere conducive to successful connections and interchange.

He also noted down a concept taken from Wolf's work….

- LEAST – ACTION PATHWAYS – As Wolf says, "Anything that becomes habitual eventually becomes unconscious" This becomes our "least –action pathways" that we stay in unconsciously and through which we observe the world. Wolf argues that at the quantum level, the action of a path can change, depending on the observer of that path. This seemed to fit with the creation of a consensus reality. So to break out of this thinking, new pathways needed to be created.

- 'BEING PRESENT' – This was something that Douglas had started to be conscious of through his work with Lise, and his meditation practice had assisted him to keep his energy focused on the 'here and now.' His open-eyed meditation as he gazed at the horizon had given him a marvellous feeling of 'just being.' It is so obvious a concept and yet so difficult to stay with as we are sometimes 'haunted' by our past and afraid of what lies before us.

Douglas had begun to realise that one of the major difficulties we had in overcoming challenges and making changes was that we were entrained to work almost exclusively through left brain thinking* and thereby use only half of our available consciousness. We attempt to address irrational challenges with our rational brain only, rather than use our imaginative or mystical realm to resolve such issues. Most of the fears that we experience in our everyday lives are irrational, he had argued with himself. Often small unnoticed fears, as he had observed and discussed during his dream. The answers to his challenges couldn't be resolved solely through the left brain

---

* Part of Roger Sperry's Nobel prize winning research on the split thinking functions of the right and left brain, the left being the logical /rational function and the right, the creative / imaginative function. This in itself appears to be the outcomes of a 'left brain' researcher!

thinking either of himself or off his colleagues. He had to find ways of inviting his colleagues to touch the irrational. Work, or more effectively, play with their magical and imaginative selves. He knew he was unlikely to 'sell' his ideas by overtly attempting to persuade his colleagues that we can work with other dimensions other than the three dimensional world that we have been trained to experience – our 'least–action consensus reality'. He would have to 'call in' his own imaginative powers to achieve what he wanted. He smiled again to himself and felt an inner confidence and excitement at the prospect of the challenges ahead. He noticed that his previously held fears had, at least for the moment, dissipated.

Chapter Eleven

Integrating the Learnings

"Before enlightenment
chopping wood
carrying water,
After enlightenment
Chopping wood
Carrying water."

Zen Proverb

So what is it I want? He decided to begin the process of synthesising his experiences, developing awareness and knowledge to make it possible to integrate and ground these back into his working life.

He had already set out the 'Rules' or 'Agreements' that he would want to build his culture around as well as identify his determinants of success.

As he relaxed into his thinking he jotted down what could be the three pillars on which to build the business...

- Culture
- Behaviour
- Performance

He liked the look and sound of these three

foundational elements and felt that they were solid enough to start the selling process.

He was aware that creating a productive Culture in his business was crucial to achieving what he wanted. This was the background against which all else would take place.

Then there was 'Behaviour'. Difficult to isolate from the Culture as behaviour affected the culture, and vice versa he thought. So yes, this would be the next 'pillar'. Behaviour would embrace the way people interacted and dealt with challenges and conflict. It would relate to emotional intelligence and management style and the type of relationships that were developed across the business. It was almost all consuming, he thought, embracing every aspect of our business lives.

Finally 'Performance'. Douglas saw this very much as the 'Outcome' and the other two, the 'Process.' Time and energy had to be directed towards business performance, and this would also be mightily affected by the culture and behaviour within the business.

His mind started to race on to how each of these could be developed, so he made a few keynotes and decided to leave the rest until he met up with Lise again.

He sat back in his seat and closed his eyes reabsorbing the energy and magic he had experienced on his Peruvian adventure.

* * *

"Your eyes haven't stopped sparkling since you came back!" Pat, Douglas's wife sat down beside him and gave him a hug. "It's marvellous to see you so happy and content and, of course, wonderful to have you back!"

Pat had tried to free herself up from her work to travel with Douglas, but had been unable to do so at short notice.

"You know I would have loved to have shared your experiences with you in Peru, and yet, I think it's probably for the best that you had time on your own to absorb the benefits of this trip and reflect on your future challenges at 'Silver Waters.'

Douglas smiled. He still loved Pat very much and was always amazed at how insightful and understanding she could be.

"I understand your point of view and to some extent agree with you. I don't think your presence would have diminished the benefits of my adventure; it would simply have changed the nature of the experience, and enhanced it in many ways. Next time we will definitely go out together. I will take great pleasure in sharing the delights of that fabulous country."

Pat gave Douglas another hug and kissed him on his cheek.

"So what was it that you found so special about the country and about your experience?"

Douglas had guessed that this would be a question that many people would ask him on his return. Especially as he was so thrilled about what he had experienced.

"Mmmm… you know, I've been attempting to rehearse my reply to that question since I left Peru, and I think the answer most people would want is a logical rational appraisal of the tangible benefits I have attained."

"So how are you going to answer it?" Pat leaned back into her half of the sofa, sipped her coffee, and waited expectantly.

"I feel as if parts of me have opened up for the first time in my life, as if my inner self has truly expanded and is filling me up. The energy that I felt and absorbed from the mountains and rivers, from the lakes and forests, from the sun and the wind, from the sacred sites was palpable. It was as if I could touch it, smell it, taste it. It is no wonder that the Incas considered the mountains, or Apus as they call them, to be Gods, and that they are still revered and are still called on by the shamans during ceremonies. I loved the openness, friendliness, and connectedness of the people, especially away from cities like Lima. There isn't the self-centredness or cynicism that seems to pervade our culture. I was thrilled to take part in the shamanic ceremonies that were offered to us. To watch these dedicated people perform their rituals with great care, great power and humility, and yet with a lightness of touch and sense of humour which made the whole experience so appealing."

Douglas paused to sip his coffee and to reflect further on his experiences.

"I was amazed at how their ancient traditions had survived for centuries, and that many of them were still carried out by a large proportion of the population. Despite the fact that their colonial masters oppressed them, they have managed to retain these traditions and their connections with the universal energy and power available to us all. I feel more grounded and centred than ever before, and now really understand what these mean!"

"You mean you didn't before?" Pat quizzed him, interested that this was something new for him.

"Yes and no. Through my work with Lise, I did begin to understand their importance, especially in staying in the present, the here and now. And I have worked with the concepts through my meditation practice. In Peru, however, I really and truly experienced the feeling of being grounded – allowing gravity to take its course and let me feel myself into the ground. And in turn, feel the energy of the ground under my feet. I think also that the healing ceremonies the shamans performed for us 'cleaned' up my energy – my heavy energy, and encouraged me to attract and work with the refined energy."

Douglas had spent some time previously explaining to Pat the various ceremonies and rituals in which they had participated so she understood what he was talking about.

"Because we spend so much in our everyday lives in our heads – in our rational, analytical mind – we lose our attachment to our body-mind. We forget that it is through our bodies that we experience the world. And by being constantly in our head, we are driven by the unconscious babble of our self-dialogue. I have found, quite dramatically, that when I'm challenged by my thoughts, I can change my focus to my centre or 'quosquo' as the Andeans would refer to it, and dissolve any negative emotion which I'm experiencing. Negative emotion is 'old' emotion, 'old' fears and attachments. By being 'in my body,' and grounded, I can stay quite clearly in the present and experience life in the moment."

"This is something which very few people experience. When quizzed, people will always indicate that, for example, the emotion of anxiety is felt in their body – usually in their stomach. It's the same with all our emotions – it is our bodies which monitor our thoughts and give us feedback on how we are 'feeling.' And yet, when experiencing a negative emotion, people will normally attempt to rationalise it in their mind! If only they would come into consciousness and work with the body-mind connection, they would begin to 'heal' themselves. I've talked to you before about Fred Alan Wolf's work?" Douglas looked for confirmation from Pat. She nodded her agreement.

"The beauty of his work is that it integrates the tangible with the intangible. The scientific (left brain) and the magical (right brain). In the imagination, he says, there is no distinction between the mind and the body. The body, he continues, responds to the mind, and the body in turn, cultivates the mind. He had noticed also that the shamans were able to use their power of imagination in a much more powerful and meaningful way than we can."

"Is that all?!" Pat was impressed with the clarity of Douglas's explanation, and asked the question with tongue in cheek.

"I think that a major difficulty in explaining the benefits of such an experience is, once again, that most people expect a black and white answer. For example, I went to Peru, and I benefited in x,y and z ways... and now I can... you know what I mean?"

Pat nodded.

"My feeling is that the benefits will keep on emerging as I face the upcoming challenges at 'Silver Waters' – like a slow release mechanism. It will be in the moment, as I have experienced before, that I will realise I have changed, grown, as I find myself handling a challenge in a more effective way."

"So what are your plans for your new 'baby'?" Douglas had always considered 'Guardian Angel' to be his 'baby.'

"I've already started through my notes made during my trip and on my return journey. I intend to redraft them and then review them with Lise."

Pat winced a little inside. In some ways she would have been better pleased if he had wanted to review these with her, but realised the impact that Lise had had on Douglas's life so far. And would, no doubt, continue to do so.

Chapter Twelve

The Integration Continues

*"When you are inspired by some great purpose, some
extraordinary project, all your thoughts break their
bonds."*

Patajali (1-3BC)

Douglas had spent his first day back catching up
on the most pressing issues that had arisen while
he was away. He was a bit disappointed that his
colleagues had not progressed or dealt with certain
items during his absence. But before moving into
judgemental mode, he reflected on his part in the
process, and smiled to himself. An indication of my
own personal learnings, he thought.

He had spent half an hour each with his most
senior colleagues so that he was up-to-date on all
current issues.

He had worked well into the evening on that first
day, as he had arranged to meet with Lise on the
following afternoon, and he wanted to 'clear the
decks' as well as he could, before moving into firstly
into reflection mode, and then onto planning mode.

He sat back in his chair at the end of this long day
with a myriad of thoughts and ideas running through

his mind. He resisted the temptation to fall into the habit of thinking and / or saying that it felt as if his trip to Peru was well in the past.

"Feels as if I've never been away." was a well-worn comment used by people back from holiday. On the contrary, he felt he had brought a bit of Peru back with him – something that would stay with him forever.

"What a transformation." he thought. "From traditional, 'hard nosed,' down-the-line business man, to....to what?" The transformation had started with his initial work with Lise and had carried on through their current association and his life changing experience in Peru. He had always considered himself to be strong but had begun to see that his apparent strength was through his previous attachment to consensus reality about how senior business executives are supposed to behave. He was also very aware that his developing approach to business (started whilst running 'Guardian Angel') was initially much more challenging, as he would not be acting out to conform to others' preconceived expectations. He had become challenged by the lack of progress that had been made in organisational life. Despite the technological advancements, MBAs, new learning opportunities etc, little had really changed throughout the twentieth century. In fact, as he had observed before, new technology was now being used to support processes and practices which had been introduced under the name of 'Scientific Management' in the nineteenth century. In call centres and administrative sections of life companies, in telesales and intermediary sales, people are now 'supervised' by technology – their every action timed and recorded to check to see how long they have spent on a task or a call, carrot and stick methods used to 'motivate' them. His experiences in Peru, however, had given him an inner strength on which he could call when the inevitable challenges arose.

'Collective responsibility' was a concept that had been filling his consciousness of late. Related not only to organisational life, but also to society in general. His ideas around this concept had in fact developed as a result of his increased consciousness and curiosity of the world around him, and his behaviour of people in everyday life. Why, he had thought, can we not solve the problem of litter in our streets, of people speeding in their cars in built up areas, and, of course, of drink driving? Why do people who are not disabled still park in disabled parking spaces or don't return shopping or baggage trolleys to the proper place? Although some of these may appear trivial, they were all part of the symptoms of what Douglas considered to be self-absorption, a sort of 'look after number one, and to hell with the rest' attitude. These symptoms are expressed in organisations through the 'not my job' syndrome, or, as is often observed, people working in 'silos' with no awareness or concern of how their actions affect their colleague or customers.

"If I can crack that nut in 'Silver Waters' I'll be a happy man." Douglas smiled at the thought, then realised that his self dialogue was pretty ineffective in creating the intention he desired.

"How about ......when I crack this nut..." He folded his arms and nodded his head in satisfaction, and wondered how many other times he still processed his intentions inappropriately. One of his favourite quotes attributed to Johan Wolfgang Von Goethe, but actually written by a Scottish climber called William Hutchison Murray, always brought him back to consciousness about the importance of intention and commitment. He had it sitting framed on his desk, and knew of one successful businessman who used it as a screen saver and as his key to successful business strategy.

He read it to himself once again....

"Until one is committed, there is hesitancy, the chance to draw back, always ineffectiveness, concerning all acts of initiative (and creation), there is one elementary truth, the ignorance of which kills countless ideas and splendid plans: that the moment one definitely commits oneself, then providence moves too. A whole stream of events issues from the decision, raising in one's favour all manner of unforeseen incidents, meetings and material assistance, which no person could have dreamt would have come their way.

Whatever you can do or dream you can, begin it. Boldness has genius, power and magic in it!"

Although the final couplet was written by Goethe, Douglas had been quietly pleased to find that it was a fellow Scot who had written the majority of this powerful piece. And one who shared his surname. Whoever it was, Douglas – in common with others who had read and absorbed its meaning – had found its message to be relevant to any aspect of his life to which it was applied.

He knew that his greatest challenge was ahead of him – to translate his thinking and findings into practical everyday action which people can understand and work with. He had to find ways of bringing that vibrant energy and magic he had experienced both in Peru, and when he was transforming 'Guardian Angel' with Lise's help, into the every day life of 'Silver Waters.' He would need her insights and guidance over the coming months.

Chapter Thirteen

"The Way Ahead"

"Invest in preparedness, not in prediction."

Nassim Nicholas Taleb

Douglas had left the following afternoon free to spend with Lise and had spent a busy morning further updating himself and meeting with his key colleagues.

"And how is our Peruvian shaman today?"

Douglas looked up from his laptop as Lise entered the room and stood in front of his desk in mock humility.

Douglas closed his laptop down and came round from behind the desk to give Lise his now customary hug. They walked across to the window and sat down on the comfortable leather seats that he used for informal meetings.

Lise was sitting on the edge of her seat in anticipation of Douglas's interpretation of his adventure in Peru.

"So how was it?" she asked.

Douglas had a sense that she may know more than he did about his experience in Peru, but put the thought to the back of his mind.

He sat back and related his experiences to her in as much detail as possible, punctuating the story with some of the photographs he had taken during the journey.

"Are there any themes which ran through your learnings?" Lise asked when Douglas had finished.

"Themes?" Douglas sat back to think. He had outlined his experience as he had done with Pat, articulating what he had felt he had achieved as a result of the journey.

"Any standouts?" Lise prompted him.

"Energy definitely!" He finally decided.

"How we absorb or generate it. How we use it. How we transmit it. How we can be affected by others energy, and how we can release the heavy energy or hucha that I explained."

"Also reciprocity or ayni in Quechua, or community as I translate it." He continued.

"And munay, or love, a feeling of selflessness."

"But to distil my experiences and learnings down to three themes would really be a great disservice to the whole journey. There was so much to take from it, I expect the learnings to continue over the coming months and years."

"Now that you're back in your 'real' world of work, how are you going to translate your learnings into practical outcomes, if, of course, you feel you want to!"

"Yes, I definitely do, as well as my personal development there is so much, I believe, I can translate into the world of work to assist in creating productive and successful businesses."

"Any ideas on that at this stage?"

"Well, firstly and interestingly, I discovered that my very conscious dream I had with Sam, who guided me through the organisational chamber of wounds and the chamber of contracts mirrored the ancient shamanic process of soul retrieval. This has helped me put the outcomes of the dream into perspective in relation to my developments of the culture at 'Silver Waters.'"

Lise nodded with interest, a signal which Douglas interpreted as an indication that she knew this all along.

"And why wouldn't she?" he thought.

"Indeed!" Lise surprised Douglas again. He still often forgot about her special powers to read thoughts amongst many other special gifts.

"In soul retrieval a shaman will journey on your behalf into the under-world, to retrieve and/or repair aspects of ourselves which we have suppressed or detached from, and with which it will be of benefit for us to reconnect. They visit four chambers, the first two of which are the chamber of wounds, and the chamber of contracts. In soul retrieval, these relate to our own lives. In my dream they related to organisations."

"Wow!" Lise showed her pleasure at Douglas's discovery.

"Wow indeed! How my unconscious mind worked that one out beats me."

"More powerful than we can imagine. Is that not what they say?"

"Certainly in this case!" Douglas had really come alive, something which always occurred in the company of Lise. He reckoned it was her energy that helped him to raise his.

"Yes, so the first link is through my soul retrieval dream and the new contracts which I created as a result of it. Although referred to as contracts, I think they form a great basis for our values linked in with what we believe in and how we agree to work together. This is a starting point; I intend to involve my colleagues in creating these as a basis for the development of our culture. If you remember, these included…

…'US.com'

…'Build Trust and Support'

…'Develop US.com Networks as Business Communities'

…'Involve and Engage all Colleagues, Customers, Partners and

…'Solutions, Solutions, Solutions'

…'Uplift and Inspire the Spirit…'

"Since creating these new contracts, I've extended my thinking around what will make us truly different." Douglas paused and took a deep breath.

"Well, go on!" Lise was fascinated to hear what was coming next.

"It centres on the concept of 'Collective Responsibility' and ideas that I have been playing with for some time."

Lise smiled, remembering Arie de Gues' quote that 'to play is to learn'. (from The Living Company, Arie de Gues)

Douglas explained his developing concept of 'Collective Responsibility' as succinctly as he could, relating it to the Andean concept of anyi and reciprocity.

"I like it," she said, "and how will you translate this into something which will work in practical terms?"

"Poacher turned gamekeeper then?" Douglas laughed.

"You'll get plenty of this once you start implementing your ideas."

Douglas nodded in agreement and stood up beside a flipchart that he had strategically placed beside him.

"Before we know it, you'll be a consultant with your ubiquitous flip chart and power point presentations!"

Douglas gave Lise a knowing look.

He wrote 'Collective Responsibility' at the top of the page.

"As I see it, a 'Collective Responsibility' business culture, effectively managed, will lead to 'Collective Success' and ultimately 'Collective Rewards.' Voila!"

He stood back to view his work...

"Don't you think it might be better as a circular process?" Lise suggested, exchanging places with Douglas.

"What about..."

"When this process works well, the Collective

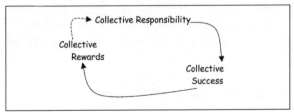

Rewards will fuel further Collective Responsibility. Yes?"

"Yes, I think that's what I meant, only my consultancy skills are not as well honed as yours!"

"Touché!" Lise laughed in response.

"And some of the practicalities or building blocks of 'Collective Responsibility'?" she inquired.

They changed places again.

"In a business context – because, as you know, I believe this to be a societal concept – this will mean…" He started writing again on the flipchart….

- Accepting a salary or wage from a business equates with accepting 'Collective Responsibility'.

"Does that not depend on how valued the person feels?" Lise interrupted.

"Absolutely! The business's responsibility will be to create a climate in which people accept this 'contract.'" He continued writing…

- It means taking responsibility for our influence and effect on…
  - our business outcomes
  - our colleagues
  - our customers
  - our suppliers
  - our community
  - society at large

"Are we talking about ethics here?" Lise quizzed Douglas again.

"This will be inherent within our values. Ethical and ecological will be two key elements of our values."

He started writing again…

(Collective responsibility…)

- Means being open to and accepting feedback from anyone within our business community.

"In other words," Douglas continued this time

pre-empting Lise's question, "everyone is encouraged to take an interest in the whole business, not simply their precious domain. They also have to be prepared to listen to colleagues who may have suggestions for them to improve their area of work. Remember one of the 'contracts' was 'Solutions,' 'Solutions,' 'Solutions!'" We will not be looking for negative feedback, rather for solutions. So often in business people become so precious about their area that they refuse to accept feedback or ideas from other people working in other areas. We will also look at creating simple mechanisms to allow individuals to progress an idea or initiative that will develop the business."

"Sounds as if you could be revisiting concepts of quality teams and the like."

"I'd rather we created something innovative which assisted us in achieving long term success rather than a short term initiative. I have some ideas for this and hope that my colleagues will contribute to these developments."

"We have a fantastic example of both innovation and community-based working in the field of technology in the open-source web server community."

"Moving into the world of high tech now by the sounds of it!"

"Definitely, in my appreciation that we must be at the forefront of technological solutions for our business in the global community in which we operate. And, I've just read Thomas L. Friedman's 'The World is Flat,' in which he explains the technological advances that have been made particularly over the last 5-10 years. The example to which I was referring is where a source code – which is the underlying programming instructions which make a piece of software work – is made freely available online to anyone who can make a contribution to improving it. The only stipulation is that you make your improvements available to the wider community. They call this uploading. Friedman gives the example of the web server called Apache which was created and developed within an online community and on which IBM built its e-commerce software and Amazon.com runs its website. All developed for free within a community of what Friedman calls 'computer geeks'. A great example that people can work in communities even if we have never met our colleagues!"

"So you can't really afford to have people who are resisting change and restricting your opportunities for development."

"Exactly! And I particularly appreciated Friedman's observation that when we ensure we have the most up-to-date workflow tools, then so will most of our competitors. And he reminds us that 'you still have to have a unique product or service to offer. And for that you often need to develop a unique way to apply information technologies to your core value proposition,' what do you think?"

"So far, so good. I will be interested to hear in due course some of the mechanisms which will be used to effect your vision of the business you desire."

Douglas flipped the flipchart back to Lise's development of his first illustration and added 'Our Business' in the middle…

Douglas stood back to admire his work. Lise nodded, "You are obviously very pleased with yourself and excited by what you've just added. Are you going to let us into your secret?"

"Yes, of course! Just taking my time!" Douglas was so thoroughly absorbed in this process, Lise could see his energy expand as he worked.

"'Our Business' will be the main centre piece of our culture. Our aim will be to create an organisation where people truly feel that it is 'Their Business.' We won't be able to approach it in the way Andy Law at St Lukes Advertising Agency did, but I really believe it can be done! You see, 'US.com' is 'Our Business!'"

"The success of any team, or business depends on individuals accepting their personal responsibility for their own inputs and outputs. 'I.com' is the starting point for developing 'US.com' or 'Our Business,' where individuals come into consciousness about running their own 'business' i.e. their life. This was one of the first awakenings you gave me at 'Guardian Angel,' remember?"

Lise nodded, "And I see you've moved the concept into the dot.com era using 'I.com' as an individual's business – I like that! I would become Lise@I.com and you will be Douglas@I.com."

"Thanks, it's a easy concept to grasp at an intellectual level, just a little harder to put into practice!"

"Like common sense?"

"Indeed. It's always interesting to hear people interpret something as 'common sense' and then completely ignore it! So, as they accept the 'I.com' way of thinking and behaving, individuals accept responsibility for their outcomes, put aside their 'excuses' and begin to identify ways in which they can develop their 'business' i.e. themselves. In the context of 'Our Business' they will direct some of that development to developing the business.

"Working within a team and a business, individuals have two key responsibilities. Firstly to ensure their I.com contribution is effective and productive whilst taking full responsibility for that input. And secondly, to be aware of, and awakened to, their 'collective responsibility' to the team. To ensure that their actions contribute towards the 'Bigger Picture' and the aspirations of the business; that their behaviours are in line with the desired team culture and that they actively look for ways of supporting and assisting colleagues wherever possible. I want people to realise that we all have influence in the world around us. And when we have a critical mass of people who operate in this way, we can generate a significant and powerful influence in all our dealings."

"Will this include ownership of the business?"

"You mean share ownership?"

"Yes, will people be given share options?"

"Yes, that's one of the elements of 'Our Business,' and these options will be open to all after they have worked for us for twelve months. I know this has been done many times before with mixed success, but it has to be one of a raft of opportunities to create the type of culture that we desire."

Lise once again nodded her agreement.

"Culture is key to ensuring we get buy-in across the entire business. And you will see in time the innovations and initiatives we will introduce to ensure we continue to grow and expand our 'Collective Success,'"

"I like the sound of that... 'Collective Success' ...it

has a good ring to it."

"What we also have to ensure though is consistent and effective management and, as 'First, Break all the Rules' demonstrates, through their extensive research, poor managers operating in a good business culture will still produce poor results. And, that it is more common for people to leave a manager than it is for them to leave a business. This emphasises the need for consistent and continuous high quality management development. It never ceases to amaze me that many businesses, and large blue chip ones at that, ignore the importance of constantly expanding their managers' talents and capabilities as well as ensuring that the teams they are running are working together effectively to achieve their full potential."

"You got that one of your chest!"

"It's certainly close to my heart!" Douglas replied with a large grin on his face.

"So you've looked at your soul retrieval dream outcome and your development of the Andean concept of Anyi, what about your other reflections or learnings from your Peruvian adventure? What about energy?"

Douglas wasn't quite sure where to start with this.

"Anywhere will do!" Lise suggested.

Douglas smiled and shook his head, reminding himself once again to be careful about what he was thinking.

"In the 'western' world we take energy for granted, in that few people are aware of how they generate, and use or abuse it. People may complain about their low energy and yet do little to increase it. We are also generally unaware of how we fight with others for their energy and how others can steal ours. It's one of the very significant sections of The

Celestine Prophecy where this fight for energy is explained. In eastern tradition Chi is of central importance as is Kawsay in the Andean world. When someone is unwell, a shaman will work with the person's energy, and will recognise disease within their energy body."

"Unfortunately many of our organisations are low energy organisations. Those who run them may have a driving ambitious energy and yet fail to tap into the potential energy of those who work for them. And because fear is still used as a common motivator in our business, we accumulate large quantities of 'hucha', or dense energy. We forget the human spirit requires to be refreshed and revitalised on a regular basis."

"So are you saying that it is the responsibility of an organisation to refresh and revitalise their people's energy? What about I.com?"

"I think it's a shared responsibility – a 'collective responsibility' Douglas paused to emphasise the connection to Lise, who smiled back in acknowledgement. "When we assist people to operate from an I.com mentality, we will expect them to be aware of their personal responsibility to direct their energies in a productive way, and understand ways of generating and protecting their energy."

"Any ideas how to do this?" Lise was now consistently pushing Douglas to demonstrate the pragmatic elements of his plans.

"Yes, I have a number of ideas which will emerge in due course. What I want to add at this point is that the organisation also has a responsibility firstly not to abuse people's energy, and secondly to provide opportunities for refreshing and refocusing their energy. The organisation and the individual have to be interdependent – like any successful relationship – to achieve the collective success that we are seeking."

"Our challenge with this will be in providing these opportunities and learnings without coming across as too weird or 'new-agey.'"

"How did it come across in Peru?"

"The interesting thing about this was that the shamans and other teachers worked almost totally without ego, were matter-of-fact and had an impish sense of humour. This contrasts with the often ego-driven, self-absorbed approach that some adherents in 'our world' adopt."

"One of the most profound differences in how we live our lives compared to the Andeans, is that we have almost completely lost our connections with the energies of the natural world. In contrast, they recognise the benefits of reconnecting with the energy of the mountains, the rivers, and the forests, of the natural world that surrounds us. The energy I felt in Peru was palpable – I could feel it, especially in the sacred sites we visited, but probably even more so from the proximity of the mountains. Opening to that energy was both energising and uplifting. I'm not, of course, saying that no one in our culture appreciates this or experiences it. It's why people climb mountains, hill walk and sail for example. It's why I love taking my dog Tara for peaceful walks by the river. I now realise more clearly why this is beneficial. It is in itself a type of healing process, as is meditation, Tai Chi and other forms of 'managing' our energy and indeed our emotions."

"So energy is quite important for you?" Lise's tongue in cheek question amused Douglas, and he also noticed how skilful she was in using these simple questions – with a hint of humour – to keep his energy high. Something to remember for future use he thought.

"Yes, I believe so." Douglas responded in a deadpan manner before bursting into a smile. "Undoubtedly so and crucial to the type of culture and dynamic business that we will build at 'Silver Waters.' You wait and see…!"

"And so to love!" Lise continued

"Ah, indeed!" Douglas responded grinning from ear to ear at her introduction to one of the Andean 'stances' known as Munay.

"One of the first people I met in Peru was a guide or paquo called Julio who told me that the most important element in Peruvian culture was Munay. It complements the concept of anyi, probably preceding it. In translation it means love from the heart, a sense of selflessness and empathy for others or for the world around us."

"The antithesis of the fear and anger that we are seeing more in more in our society?" Lise suggested.

"Absolutely! It seems to be everywhere, on the roads, the streets, with politicians, sportsmen and their coaches. I even heard recently of pool lane rage in swimming pools! You know in Cusco there were seven and eight year old children selling postcards and trinkets on the streets, who asked politely where I came from, then were able to tell me the name of my capital city Edinburgh and, even if I didn't' buy anything, went on their way with a smile and a wave."

"How wonderful!"

"You generate that feeling of munay, of great empathy and so indeed does Pat, my wife."

"And you do too now." Lise replied smiling at Douglas.

"What do you mean now?" Douglas's attempt at feigned anger fell on stony ground.

"I think you will agree that when we met at first, you weren't projecting that feeling within your business dealings. Yes, of course, you had that capacity within you, but had dampened it down to conform to the consensus reality of organisational life. Do you remember reading 'Sophie's World' by Jostein Gaarder?"

"Yes, quite some time ago now."

"Do you remember the mythical philosopher, Alberto's description of how consensus reality works?"

"Remind me." Douglas had been very taken with the book at the time of reading, and wasn't now able to remember its full details.

"He describes our experience of being in this amazing world as if a magician had pulled a gigantic rabbit out of his magic top hat, with each of us starting out our life at the top of a piece of fur on the rabbit's back."

Douglas nodded and smiled as he began to recall the metaphor.

"At the top of the piece of fur, we look out at the world with wonder, amazement and joy, interested in every small detail or object we come across. Highly inquisitive, as parents will tell you as they deal with the constant 'why,' 'who,' 'what,' 'where' and 'how' questions, like 'where do we come from?', 'how did we get here?', 'who is God?' and so on. Most parents have long since stopped asking these questions, and divert their child's attention away from such matters."

"And hence stop asking questions and accept the norm?"

"Yes – as Alberto says through our social conditioning, we start to slip down our piece of fur into consensus reality, into the deeper conditioning. If you think about it, what do all parents, and probably especially, grandparents want to see their young children doing?"

Douglas shook his head, not quite understanding what she was getting at.

"When people look into a pram at a young child, what do they encourage them to do?"

"Smile or laugh, I guess?"

"Exactly! So for the first few years of our lives, people want us to laugh and have fun. You don't hear parents telling their friends that they're so proud of their child because he/she is such a miserable little sod! But at some point in the future things start to change, and we're told to 'get serious' and to 'take that smile off your face.'"

Douglas nodded as he remembered teachers in his primary school days telling him that they'd soon take that smile off his face, which at that time meant being belted on the hands with a leather belt.

"So, in a rather round-a-bout way, I was pointing out that you have now allowed your true self to show through and are confident enough in yourself to let your work colleagues see this part of you as well."

"Thank you, I appreciate that, although I still find this a challenge at times, especially when faced with a Board who still operate through consensus reality."

"You challenge them!"

"Indeed. And a challenge I have chosen to accept. If I hadn't then I would still be working for Universal! Translating the concept or 'stance' as the Andeans call it, of munay and others into everyday working life is the big challenge."

"Any ideas?" Lise was keen that Douglas was able to translate his new thinking into practical action.

" I think the starting point is through our company values, which emanate from the new 'contracts' which we discussed."

Douglas switched on his laptop and assessed his Power-Point files.

"I have already outlined these to show you. The continuing challenge with this though, is firstly to ensure that I get buy-in to these values, from colleagues across the business, and I'm quite prepared to adapt and adjust them to achieve that purpose. And secondly, to ensure that they can be incorporated into the day-to-day life of the business. So often we see 'Our Values' statements on the walls of reception areas of businesses more to create a company image than to establish working practices that are informed through the stated values. In reality few people pay much attention to these statements. Our challenge at 'Silver Waters' is to embed these values into the life and work of our business!" Again Douglas emphasised 'Our Business' as the central pillar on which the culture will be built.

"Let's have them then!" Lise sat back in anticipation and also in admiration at the change in Douglas's outlook and focus since they first met. He definitely had exceeded her initial expectations of the speed of change that she had anticipated.

Douglas brought up the first slide...

'At Silver Waters we value ...'

'Every contribution to Our Business.'

"This will be seen through our reward system, share options, colleague benefits, recognition etc." Douglas explained. "I have a whole raft of mechanics which I want to 'sell' to my colleagues."

He brought up the next slide..

'We value…'

'The Process of Reciprocity'.

"The Andean concept of anyi, of 'community' translates into 'Collective Responsibility.' Removing the 'silo' mentality will help to make this possible." Douglas explained.

"And the next…?"

'We value…'

'The human spirit and its ability to cope with adversity.'

"Wow, that's not one you'll see too often in company reception areas!" Lise was impressed and also concerned that Douglas could be challenged quite strongly about some of these values from colleagues who hadn't achieved his level of awakening or understanding.

"I know I'm taking a bit of a risk with some of these." Douglas replied picking up Lise's concerns intuitively. "And I will work hard to demonstrate their practical application within the business. We will create a range of opportunities where our people can re-energise and re-focus to deal with the day-to-day challenges they face. None may be unique in themselves, but I do believe the package of offerings will be unique."

He flicked over to the next page…

'We value…'

'Trust – in ourselves and each other.'

"We will foster open communication within our teams and across our teams and provide opportunities for our people to voice their views and express their fears in open forms. We know this will take time to achieve, and, of course, I know by now, the part that I play in making this a reality."

And the next...

'We value...'

'Innovation as a means of generating continuous growth and Collective Success.'

"I think you'll see how interdependent these are, and how they relate to 'Our Business' culture. In this case, you will see that by ensuring 'Collective Success' leads to 'Collective Rewards', then people will be motivated to look for ways to increase our success through innovation. We will also have a policy to ensure that innovations are able to be reviewed openly and followed through effectively."

"What will you have – innovation enforcers?"

"Not exactly!" Douglas smiled at her tongue-in-cheek question." "We will need a mechanism to ensure that firstly, people can be confident of being listened to, and then will have the support of colleagues to see it through. Having Innovative Co-ordinators may well be a possibility as long as we don't begin to create a mountain of red tape procedures around the process. And on to the next value" Douglas brought the next slide up...

'We value ...'

'Feedback from all sources.'

"I remember reading many years ago that 'Feedback was the Breakfast of Champions' a view to which I have always been in agreement, in principle, but can recall many times in the past when I have resisted it. The problem within many organisations is that the majority of feedback is delivered and received as criticism and blame for mistakes. And I've already pointed out how defensive people can be when feedback is offered from outside their domain or department. A key element of 'Our Business' culture will be an openness to feedback from colleagues, suppliers, customers and community with an agreed 'contract' to respond productively to any feedback received. It's tough medicine for all of us to listen to feedback which doesn't currently fit with our own map of the world, and it's one we're going to have to accept in order to achieve the success we desire."

Lise nodded in agreement.

"The last two values are closely inter-linked, the latter being a tougher 'sell' to some within the business."

'We value…'

'Collective Success.'

"A concept we have examined previously, but when set against the final value, challenges what we normally mean when we talk of business success."

"Like return on investment, shareholder or stakeholder returns, revenues and profits and so on?" suggested Lise.

"Yes, that and a few other accepted measures that are the norm, and please don't misunderstand me, these will still be very important measures for the business, they just won't be the only ones. To put this in context, let's look at my final value…

'We value…'

'A higher purpose over and above making money.'

"So, I'm still well aware that we require to

continue to make money, but that we also do value other elements of organisational life over and above the monetary one."

"So how would you describe 'a higher purpose' if challenged?" Lise asked.

"In organisational terms 'a higher purpose' relates to our consciousness that we are not an isolated mechanism to make money, and in the process have found a convenient way of doing so. It is about creating an internal environment in which people can thrive, realising the impact that our business has on these individuals, and in turn, how this affects our communities, our society and our planet. It is about developing a consciousness of 'social responsibility' and involving our colleagues in the ways in which we can contribute to our society as a whole. Hence as my previous observation that the last two values are inextricably linked, 'Collective Success' will relate to a wider purpose than accumulation for its own sake. This is starting to emerge more powerfully with many companies implementing a Corporate and Social Responsibility Policy and Programme, although I have doubts over some of their motivation."

"You have a formidable job ahead Douglas."

"And there's more! There's another couple of elements which have impressed me on my travels and in my reading which I would want to incorporate into my future work at 'Silver Waters'."

"Go on then!" Lise was fascinated by Douglas's enthusiasm to turn his experiences into practical action back in his 'real world'.

"The first is the idea of ritual, and before you begin to think that I'm going to dress up in robes and perform an Inca ritual back in the business, then think again!" They both laughed loudly at the thought of Douglas robed up at a Board meeting.

"So how can you see this idea of ritual being used in everyday business life?"

"Well, if you take management meetings, for example, we've already seen how sterile and predictable these can be. We've also seen how switched off people can be, even to the extent of working on their laptops and blackberries during a meeting. We, in the 'western' world have a different concept of ritual than traditional cultures, in that we think of them as something – some activity- we do in a similar way on a regular basis. Some people, for example, would refer to their morning routine of showering and breakfasting as a morning ritual, rather than simply a repetitive routine that helps to ground them into a new day. Useful in its own right, and yet not what would be considered a true ritual. In traditional cultures a ritual is an event that is created for a specific purpose and in itself will be unique. There may be similarities from previous rituals, but the overall experience will be unique."

"So where does the idea of 'ceremony' fit into this, as you have referred to these in your travels?"

"Ceremony would relate more to the 'routine' activity. In ceremony there is usually a pattern of activity to follow such as a religious or military ceremony or even at Christmas time when the 'man of the house' carves the turkey. And just to complicate matters, there may be elements of ceremony within a ritual, in say the starting or finishing activities."

"So how does all that relate back to your starting point of meetings?"

"Ah yes! Meetings. I was rather enjoying pontificating on rituals and had forgotten where I started. But just before I relate these ideas to business meetings, a thought has occurred to me that each day in our life could be viewed as a ritual."

"You mean with bits of ceremony or routine and bits of unique experiences."

"Yes, I think that's what I mean, and in fact, this will link back with my final observation."

"In what way?"

"Let me deal with the first issue first, otherwise I could get lost in the image of thoughts and ideas that seem currently to be springing into my active mind!"

"Ok, meetings it is!"

"Yes. Getting back to meetings and, in particular, how we can bring them to life, make them worthwhile experiences."

Lise interjected, "Let me get the ball rolling. We've all probably heard, or maybe even said, 'these meetings are a complete waste of time.' Agreed?"

"Definitely heard, but of course, never said!" Douglas nodded, and smiled.

"A good question to ask in this context is whether the person could show you a 'meeting.' That is, physically bring a 'meeting' into a room." Lise continued.

Douglas looked a bit bemused.

"Not quite with you."

"Well, in linguistic terms, the word 'meeting' would be called a 'nominalisation' – which means it can actually mean anything you want it to mean because it doesn't exist as an actual object. It is an abstract concept. So, when the person who made the above statement about meetings being a waste of time agrees that a meeting doesn't really exist, you can ask them 'who then wastes time at meetings?' "

"I get it. This then means they have to admit that

it is themselves who wastes their time."

"And you can then coach them on helping to make meetings more productive."

"I like that!"

"And it can be done without being defensive and aggressive. It's part of what's known in Neuro Linguistic Programming (NLP) as the Meta Model. We'll do some more work on this presently."

"So, back to the drawing board!" Douglas sat forward in his seat ready to explain at last about how ritual concepts could be incorporated into meetings.

"I've already started making meetings more interesting at 'Silver Waters' introducing some of the ideas that we introduced at 'Guardian Angel.' The first thing I pay attention to is 'space.' So many meetings take place with people crammed into a small room, around a table with often no natural light. It's very unlikely that anything really productive, or especially creative, will emerge from this environment. So we have to create a 'ritual' space – a space which will be conducive to creative thinking, to building relationships, to being open with and trusting of colleagues, and to experiencing meetings as worthwhile and productive means of taking the business forward. As you know, I like a good sized open space with plenty of natural light and no tables to sit around. Some of my colleagues at 'Silver Waters' were thrown by having no tables, in particular to put their laptop on. I got some strange looks initially."

"And how is it now?"

"I've not had many meetings as yet, but my colleagues seem to be enjoying the new ideas and, have come along much better prepared than when I started. Other ways of creating a good space is by using plants and flowers – incorporating their natural energy into the room. Again, my colleagues were surprised by the flowers when we had our first meeting. Pictures, objects etc can also enhance the space, as can music, candles and incense. I have to say, the latter two will be later introductions! I also like the idea of large cushions to sit on rather than chairs. I've pinched that idea from another company I heard of who had all their board meetings seated on cushions. Changing the space we meet in is also important, to break routine. Either a different room, or a different venue, or when weather permits, an appropriate outdoor space. A friend of mine who works for a major hotel chain, for example, used to take his management team out on the Yorkshire Dales on occasions, and regularly surprised them with innovative ideas to generate enthusiasm and creativity within the business. It is really quite amazing how some businesses expect creativity, enthusiasm and energy from their people without demonstrating these traits in the way they operate the business! What is not surprising is that my friend always exceeded his targets for revenue and profits and continues to succeed now in an international environment."

"The sad thing is that even after 'hearing' information like that, many people will 'filter' it out and continue to do what they've always done!"

"Using their 'least-action-pathways,' which is a concept I'll spend a little time on later."

"And I'll encore on filters later too!" Lise always had the facility to stay quite playful without this getting in the way of what they were discussing. A skill that Douglas admired and aimed to further develop for his own purposes.

"Another element of ritual which I have begun to incorporate into my meetings, without, I may say, at the moment anyway, using the word 'ritual' – is being clear about each person's role and expected contribution to the meeting. Fostering the idea of 'Our Meeting' rather than 'My Meeting'!" This means that people come prepared and ready to contribute rather than 'waste their time' at meetings. I'd like to extend this idea further by encouraging colleagues to become involved in creating the right type of space and environment to keep us connected and productive."

"As they see the results coming from your new approaches, I'm sure that they will want to take a greater part in not only energising meetings, but creating an energising culture along the lines you have already explained. I also like the continued theme of 'Our' as you used again in the context of meetings."

"The danger with any innovation of the types we are discussing, and these are only the tip of the iceberg, is that they will be viewed as a fad, or as people will possibly say of them as the 'flavour of the month.'"

"You overcame a good deal of that though at 'Guardian Angel' by demonstrating your commitment to the changes over time, and with your added insights from that experience and from your Peruvian adventure, you will overcome any resistance at 'Silver Waters,' possibly with a little additional help from you-know-who!"

"I will, as always, welcome all the help you can give. This journey would not have happened had you not walked into my life at 'Guardian Angel.' And before we 'move off' rituals, just a footnote to remind ourselves that there will be other business activities that can be enlivened through adopting a ritualistic approach. The Induction process is one that easily springs to mind. Often a dull and boring introduction to policies and procedures, we are already looking at ways of making it more exciting as well as informative. Company conferences, open forums, in-house training and development, product launches, business feedback sessions. They will all, in time, have this treatment to assist in 'uplifting and inspiring our people.'"

"What a fabulous thought! And you had one more element to consider from your recent travels and reading?"

"Yes, we've already touched on it on one or two occasions, so this shouldn't take long."

"There's no hurry, take as much time as you want."

"Our habits, as Fred Alan Wolf describes, arise through the creation of what are known as 'least-action pathways'. By becoming conscious of the world around us, we created these pathways, and they in-turn became habits necessary for our survival. He tells us that 'anything that becomes habitual eventually becomes unconscious'. In other words we don't even notice what we are doing, or the effect we have on others. He also points out that …'in our mind we make a groove, a roadway, that we follow without thinking' and that 'people stay in their groove', even if it is uncomfortable. They don't even think about it anymore! This is our real challenge of change- to awaken people to their ' habit' and to the bigger habit that is consensus thinking. Wolf highlights this by indicating that we are usually unaware of our actions 'because our beliefs are based on past experiences and those in turn are based on the habits we have built up! He describes this as a 'self-consistent loop', a trap. I think it was yourself who told me that one of the main reasons that we find it hard to change is because we become addicted to who we think we are. Which is similar, I believe, to what Wolf is saying?"

Lise smiled and nodded in agreement.

"And that brings me to the end – for now that is – of my new thinking on how to instigate real change in our business. What do you think?"

"Very powerful and very brave of you to be prepared to step out of the norm and face up to the challenges you will have in turning these ideas into reality."

"Thanks! Yes, I know there will be people who will resist these ideas and my aim will be to both develop my skills in dealing with these, as well as avoiding a fear driven mentally which in turn, would lead me to be defensive and possibly aggressive. If one of my goals is to avoid developing a fear orientated culture in the business then it is essential that I stay clear of fear."

"Well said! And what skills do you envisage will assist you in dealing with the anticipated challenges? Perhaps we should take a look at what could lie ahead…?"

Douglas sensed that Lise was about to provide him with yet another remarkable insight, this time into the future.

"So, we're off on another mystical adventure?"

"Could be!" Lise laughed as she stood up and indicated to Douglas that they were about to commence their next journey.

Chapter Fourteen

Overcoming Resistance

"To give no trust, is to get no trust."

Lao Tzu

As they left the office they stepped into a restaurant that Douglas recognised as being a few minutes from the 'Silver Waters' headquarters building.

"We've done a bit of time travelling this time." Lise turned and smiled at Douglas as they observed a small group of his colleagues who were gathering for a meeting."

"Nothing surprises me now!" He replied shaking his head. In truth, he was still amazed, and part of him bemused by these types of experiences.

"How far into the future are we?" He asked as he noticed who was in the room. Mark Adams, the Business Development Director was there, as was his Finance Director, Stewart Reice, and Pete Fisher his HR Director, the only one of these three who didn't sit on the Board. "At least at the moment." Douglas thought, not quite sure to which moment he was referring! There was also Nigel Stevens, a non-executive Director with a background in Investment

Management and Marketing. He was an imposing figure of a man, six feet six inches tall with thick white hair and an athletic frame – a legacy from a sporting life where he had excelled at rugby and cricket and still played to a single figure handicap at golf. Despite his sixty one years, he looked at least ten years younger.

"Three months only. This is an informal gathering taking place on the morning of a Board Meeting." Lise brought him back to the 'present,' Douglas had already noted that the two female members of his senior team were not present.

"A male-only event then?" He quipped.

"Looks like it. Perhaps your female colleagues are otherwise engaged!"

"A breakfast meeting by the looks of it?"

"Yes. It's 8.00am."

The four members of the group had taken their seats at a round table, having gathered their respective breakfast items from the buffet.

"There's plenty of room at the table. Let's just sit alongside and listen in."

Douglas knew the set-up for these situations by now, understanding that he was both invisible and unable to be overheard by the other participants.

"So what is it you want from me?" Nigel Stevens was keen to get on with it. "Let me make it clear that I'm happy to listen to what you have to say, but you must realise that I will neither be party to any schemes you have in mind, and if there is anything substantial relating to Board matters, I will insist that you raise them at today's meeting. Understood?"

Douglas's three colleagues nodded in agreement. Douglas also nodded his approval, pleased to hear that Nigel was demonstrating why he had been invited onto the Board in the first place.

"We are worried that the changes which Douglas has been introducing to 'Silver Waters' will be damaging to our business."

Stewart Reice started the ball rolling. He continued, "They will, in my view, mean a huge increase in costs. The way he seems to be taking us is not the way financial businesses are run!"

"I'm not convinced by all this stuff he's been introducing about collective responsibility. If marketing cocks up, I'm not sharing the blame!" Mark Adams chipped in.

"Ouch!" Douglas thought. "I haven't made much headway there." he whispered to Lise.

"He's never been the same since he was in Peru." Pete Fisher began his contribution to proceedings.

"Well that's a positive!" Thought Douglas. "I'm glad he's noticed the difference in me."

"The problem is, if these changes don't work, we'll have to remove them." Stewart Reice continued along the cost route, as Douglas would have expected.

"It's just too big a change, it could never work." Mark Adams added in support.

"Please don't think we're totally unhappy with Douglas as our CEO. He's done some great things so far. We're just interested in your views on some of the changes he's been making." Pete Fisher introduced a more conciliatory approach to the proceedings.

"Let's go. I think we've heard enough from this scenario. Plenty of ammunition to work on I think!"

Lise was up and heading off, with Douglas hurrying along behind, not liking the thought of being stuck in a time period three months hence.

"Don't worry, Nigel deals with it magnificently. I just wanted you to have some idea of the language people use when resisting change, so that we can develop your skills to deal with it. Remember I mentioned the Meta Model earlier?"

Douglas nodded.

"Well, this stuff will help us be prepared to turn this resistance around and help everyone move forward positively and smoothly."

"Sounds good to me!"

They were now back in Douglas's office. Douglas sat down on one of his comfy chairs while Lise remained standing. She was a striking looking woman, Douglas thought. Although he had never viewed her as any thing other than a colleague initially, and latterly as a friend, he was aware of her subtle beauty and well-honed figure. If he hadn't been married and happy to be so, who knows, he had wondered. She was considerably younger than Douglas in her early thirties, and as yet unattached. She had talked briefly with Douglas about her background but was reticent about going into any great detail. She had had a few relationships in the past, but had never felt committed enough to make them long term. She seemed very content to live a maverick-style life. Douglas had offered her a position at 'Silver Waters' as a cross between an internal consultant and his executive assistant. Not the same, he had pointed out, as a personal assistant, the position on offer being more of an overall business related role. Lise had indicated that she would think about it, although she had previously hinted that she had other opportunities in the pipeline. He had never really been able to find out a great deal about her. When he did pose questions of a personal nature, she very skilfully and swiftly changed the subject. Maybe if she took the position on offer, he would be able to glean a little more information from her.

"You ready?" Lise waved her hands in front of Douglas's face.

"Ah yes, of course. Fire away!" Douglas refocused his attention back on the task in hand having quite obviously drifted off. And then realised that if she had wanted to, she could have been fully aware of the thoughts he was having. Glad that they had been mainly of a professional nature, he turned his attention back to Lise.

"So you do remember some of the work we did previously on our filters to perception?" Lise quizzed Douglas. With a sense of déjà vu, Douglas replied in the affirmative.

"Definitely! How could I forget?" His turn to have his tongue firmly in his cheek.

"Yes, I do remember," he continued "that we all interpret events differently because of our in-built filters to our perception. And that some of these filters include our values, beliefs our personal contracts about how things are supposed to be for us, our egos and so on."

"Well done!" Lise was standing beside the flip chart and ready to continue to develop Douglas's understanding of filters.

"Well thank you. I had a very good teacher!" Douglas replied in good humour. He was looking forward to hearing more.

"As you know when we observe any 'event' in the 'outside world', in our process of making meaning of the 'event', we filter the available information through our own personal filters."

Douglas nodded, as she had more or less repeated what he had said previously.

"You ever had an argument or disagreement with someone?"

"Oh, I think that's a definite yes!" It was quite some time since they had had a session like this and Douglas was once again enjoying the experience.

"And it can be frustrating when someone just can't seem to see what you are getting at, and appears to be completely convinced that their view is the only view?"

"Been there too!" Douglas nodded

"And you may recognise elements of this in the scenario which we have just watched evolve. For example, when Stewart Reice says 'this is not the way financial businesses are run,'" Douglas nodded again "Stuck in his perception of how they should run?"

"Yes exactly, and filtering out any 'new' information which does not match up with his current 'map of the world.'"

"Ah, yes." Douglas remembered this phase from his earlier work with Lise, and initially felt quite challenged by it. Thought it felt a bit too much like new-age language, but was now very comfortable using it. It was synonymous with others like 'model of the world,' 'mental models' and probably also 'mindset.' All ways of describing the fact that every individual interprets their world in a unique way.

"We all use three major filters in our process of making meaning."

She then wrote on the flipchart...

DELETIONS

GENERALISATIONS

DISTORTIONS

"So in order to make meaning, we delete certain

bits of information and generalise and distort others. We all do this to some extent, primarily to sustain our overall 'map of the world.'"

"So when Stewart made that comment, he had been doing this in order to sustain his view of how financial businesses should be run?" Douglas was back in the swing of working with Lise.

"Perfect! You learn quickly."

"Oh, I already observed, I have a good teacher!"

"Thank you, and before we look at these particular filters in detail, let's take a look at how they will relate to the process of 'pacing' that we looked at before. Remember?"

"Yes, I do, and I've found these skills hugely important in my initial dealings with colleagues at 'Silver Waters.'"

Lise turned again to the flipchart.

"So you will remember this little illustration…"

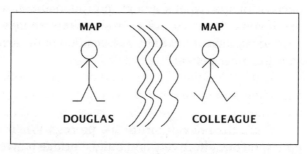

"Yes I do. The wavy line represents a river, with its width, depth, speed of flow and temperature all dependent on how different the maps are. If there is a big difference, then the gulf, represented by the river, will be wide, deep, fast flowing and very cold, a very unattractive prospect for someone to cross."

"And if you wanted to get a colleague across the great divide?"

"I'd build a bridge! Which is where pacing comes in, if I'm not mistaken?"

"No, you're absolutely right again. Pacing is the skill of bridge building."

"And we can pace body language, voice tone, volume and speed, and language patterns, which means repeating back to the other person more or less what they have said to you."

"Excellent. And there are many more ways of pacing which we can look at another time."

"The one element I felt uncomfortable using initially was pacing body language, being similar to the other person's body language. I had the feeling people would notice what I was doing."

"And did they?"

"Absolutely not! No one showed any sign that they had noticed."

"Which confirms firstly that most people are very unconscious of what's going on around them, and that if you can stay conscious in situations where you need to be, then you will be in a position of influence over the other person."

"And it definitely works. What I have noticed after time is that the other person starts to follow my movements."

"That's the second part of the process. When we pace someone effectively and build a bridge between our respective 'maps of the world,' we can actually 'lead' them back over the bridge to view our 'map.' This is called 'leading.'"

"So the whole process involves firstly pacing followed by leading. We pace the other person's 'map' and how they experience it, before 'inviting' them back across to experience ours."

Lise added to her picture on the flipchart...

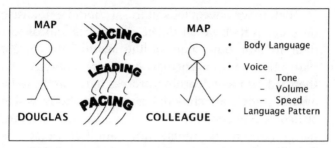

"And you may remember we also identified the word which can blow the bridge and the one that keeps it open."

"Indeed, and I have used this to good effect too in getting agreement with colleagues. Avoiding 'but' and 'however' which are discounts and disconnects in rapport building, and using 'and' to link the other person's current 'map' with an introduction to my 'map'."

"And we'll soon add the next stage in this process which is a vital addition to your 'toolbox'."

"I did, and in fact still do find it a challenge to remember to use 'and' instead of 'but'," he said emphasising the use of the word, "as I have already said, I have found it to work very effectively."

"And so to the next part of our current exploration." Lise once again turned to the flipchart and drew another of her quaint illustrations...

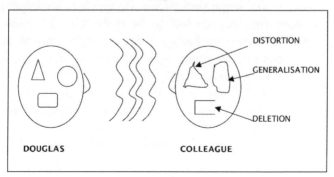

"Before we have a look at this, I should emphasise once again that we all delete, generalise and distort data to suit our 'map of the world,' or current perception of a particular issue or challenge. So there's a two way learning process here: firstly, to be aware of our attachments and associations which structure our perception of the world and secondly, being able to recognise how another person is deleting, generalising and distorting in relation to a particular issue. This helps us not to be defensive over our own take on an issue and in turn, avoiding attacking someone else's."

"I'm with you in principle with this. My challenge is in persuading people that the way forward for the business is the best way forward. As we saw in the recent scenario, my Financial Director doesn't subscribe to it, and to make matters worse, by the whole tenor of that encounter, probably doesn't feel able to tell me about his difficulty."

"That'll take a bit of time to engender the confidence in people to challenge you on your strategy for the business. You also have to remember that by skilfully dialoguing, you may be able to further enhance your strategy through the contributions from your colleagues."

"That's a big one – I'd like to take some time to look at that separately. If we are going to develop a culture that people feel to be truly 'Our Business' then we have to find a way of letting everyone contribute to our ongoing development. I have some ideas on how to do this."

"Great! I'll look forward to seeing these."

Lise drew Douglas's attention back to the flipchart.

"My illustration has taken only the heads of the

two people in the previous pacing and leading drawing. Yours and a colleague."

"And I can see I'm having some deeply meaningful thoughts." Douglas laughed, while Lise gave him a pretend look of annoyance.

"Lets imagine that the symbols in your head are your desired representation of things you want to achieve in the business. Understand?"

"So far so good. I think. Just to clarify the square, triangle and circle are representing some of my ideas for taking the business forward?"

"Yes, that 's correct. They could also represent separate parts of one idea or strategy."

"Yes, that's what I thought."

"And the symbols in your colleague's head are how they are currently representing your ideas. You'll see, for example, that they have 'deleted' one side of your 'square,' generalised your circle into an oblong-type shape and distorted your triangle."

"A rather amusing thought having my triangle distorted!"

"Behave yourself, and get serious!"

Lise gave Douglas a mock rebuke.

"A nice tie-in with our previous discussion."

"I do try!" Lise bowed mockingly to Douglas.

"Your challenge then is to recognise the language pattern which demonstrates a deletion, generalisation and distortion, pacing the pattern before asking the question which will aim to 'reclaim' that particular element."

"You'll need to give me some examples before I could understand that fully."

"What I'll do is give you some examples of what I think are the most common deletions, generalisations and distortions you will have to deal with and see how these relate to some of the language patterns your colleagues used in the scenario we viewed."

"That sounds good to me." Douglas stretched his hands above his head and took a deep breath to keep himself focused on this important work.

"Let's deal firstly with 'Deletions.' Do you remember when we first looked at the concept which we now refer to as I.com – the idea that since our life is our business, then we are all in-fact running a business?"

"Yep. I've already explained how this will be a central plank in 'Our Business'."

"And, you may remember we talked about the 'Theys, 'Thems' and 'Its', our T.T.Is which we often use as excuses when things don't work out well for us?"

"Affirmative!"

"Well these 'Theys', 'Thems' and 'Its' are examples of 'simple deletions', when for example someone says 'They don't give us enough information' or as Stewart Reice says 'They will, in my view, mean a huge increase in costs…' Remember?"

"I do indeed." Douglas replied shaking his head, still rather annoyed by the comment.

"You will begin to recognise that all the statements we will be examining will be like smokescreens, used to avoid change or to avoid touching the uncomfortable. So, to assist you in clarifying what Stewart really means, we firstly have to pace his statement as the first part of your response. Want to try?"

"How about, so 'why do you think there will be a huge increase in costs?'"

"That's not quite hitting the mark." Lise responded diplomatically.

"You mean totally wrong!" Douglas had picked up the signal pretty accurately.

"Not totally, but not far from it!"

"So what would be better?" Douglas realised the importance of developing these skills to deal with the kind of scepticism, and probably cynicism, he would most likely have to face.

"Two things to pay attention to. Firstly, using 'why' can come across as quite aggressive in an interrogative type of manner. It's better to avoid 'why' when working with the Meta Model. Secondly, you didn't actually pace Stewart's language pattern or current 'map' of this issue."

"So I should have more or less repeated back what he had said to me?"

"Correct."

"Second round, seconds out, here goes...

...'I understand Stewart, that you believe that what we are doing will lead to a huge increase in costs.' Better?"

"Perfect. I would say!"

"So, apart from Stewart realising that I had actually listened to him, are there any other reasons why we should pace the other person?"

"Yes, indeed. Any pacing technique we use will induce a light hypnotic state in the other person."

"You mean hypnotise the other person? Is that not a bit dangerous?"

"No, I didn't say hypnotise, I said it would induce a light hypnotic state. And no, it's not dangerous. Most people live a fair part of their life in a light, and sometimes not-so-light, hypnotic state!"

"I suppose a lot of our actions we take using our least-action pathways are undertaken in an unconscious slightly hypnotic state."

"Exactly. And just to put the record straight on hypnosis. No, it's not dangerous either. People still retain full control of what they will and won't do. They are simply much more open to suggestion. In hypnosis, our conscious, chattering, ego-driven, left-brained mind is quietened, and our unconscious mind opened up to suggestions."

"So why do people prance around a stage doing outrageous things when under hypnosis?"

"Because they want to. Because their unconscious minds are open to fun and to the suggestions of the hypnotist. So when we pace someone's language pattern, we quieten their attachment to their current 'map' in their conscious mind, and open up the possibility of them taking on board what you are offering them."

"So what's the next stage in the process?"

"The next stage is to tackle one of the deletions, generalisations or distortions – let's call them language patterns, which the other person is using. So if we examine Stewart's language pattern again…" they will, in my view, mean a huge increase in costs. Can you see any 'simple deletions?'"

"The proposed changes?"

"Which ones?" Lise was enjoying the process of coaching Douglas once again.

"He doesn't specify them does he?" Douglas nodded as he began to grasp what this process was about.

"No he doesn't. So could you suggest a potential response in the form of a question?"

"Well it would be around asking him to be more specific about the changes which will lead to his perceived huge increase in costs."

"Do you want to have a go at the complete

response?"

"Here goes...'I understand, Stewart, that you believe that what we are doing will lead to a huge increase in costs, and'"he emphasised this for special effect, "what specific changes will lead to this anticipated huge increase in costs?"

"Excellent!" Lise walked forward and offered Douglas a 'high five,' which he reciprocated with great pleasure.

"And there are other deletions in this statement." Lise continued, "Any ideas?"

"Well, I suppose if one looks at it, then 'huge increase' and 'costs' are both forms of deletion."

"Indeed they are. Well done."

"So when do I tackle these? At the same time as tackling 'they'?"

"You could do by asking a question which incorporates them or probably preferably to begin with, tackle them one by one."

"I could ask, after pacing of course... 'what specific changes will lead to what level of anticipated costs', or would it be better to identify the changes firstly, then ask... 'what level of costs do you anticipate being associated with the changes you have identified?'"

"They both work." Lise nodded her approval. "And for the moment I would suggest, as I said previously, that you tackle them one by one."

"I could also ask him to specify the costs to which he is referring."

"You could indeed, depending on whether or not this is clarified by the process we have already discussed. And can you see how this can help you overcome potential resistance to your proposed changes?"

"Yes. It allows me to understand exactly what I'm dealing with. It removes the smokescreen that you talked about."

"This is what it is designed to do. Bandler and Grinder, the two people who developed NLP, modelled this process on the work of a famous therapist called Virginia Satir. It's a very powerful tool in gaining clarity from someone when dealing with a complex issue."

"Sounds as if it will be an essential tool to assist me in my new journey."

"Deletions are generally considered to be the easiest pattern to clarify. Another one in this family is the 'comparative deletion', where, for example, someone will say 'it's too expensive', or 'it's too difficult' and also 'we want to get better at this', or 'I want to get fitter this year'. Can you spot these deletions?"

"The clue is in the word comparative I think?"

Douglas raised his eyebrows to reinforce that he was asking a question. Something he was well known for by his colleagues.

"Right again. So, what kind of question would suit here?"

"Something related to… 'compared with what or whom?' in the first instance, and perhaps 'better than whom?' or 'better at what?' as well as 'fitter than what?' or 'how much fitter?' Is that what you are getting at?"

Lise had forgotten what a quick learner Douglas was, allied with now being much more open to new ideas than he had been when they started out on their journey.

"Spot on once again! You do learn quickly."

"Well thank you once again for your

encouragement. Maybe it also has something to do with the skills of my teacher."

Lise nodded and smiled in acknowledgement of a compliment returned.

"And we're not finished with Stewart's language pattern."

"You mean there's more to clarify?"

"One more for now. Have you ever been faced with a comment like.. 'it'll never work?'"

"Oh, I do believe I have in my time!" Douglas responded with mock seriousness.

"Rather than look at the individual deletion or generalisations that can be identified in this short sentence, let's look at the whole language pattern... 'it'll never work.' Recognise anything in it?"

"It's very obviously a smokescreen to avoid attempting something that's different from the norm. Correct?"

"Correct! It's called 'mind reading' in Meta Model terms. It's a 'distortion.' Any ideas why they called it 'mind reading?'"

"Probably because they have extrapolated a potential outcome from a proposed change without any supportive evidence. In other words, how do they know it won't work until they've tried it?"

"And that's the basis of the question you could deliver as a response, 'How do you know this – whatever – won't work', or 'what evidence do you have which leads you to believe this won't work.'"

"Or in Stewart's case... 'what leads you to believe this will result in a huge increase in costs.'"

"Exactly! This will require Stewart to provide specific evidence for his claim, which he won't be able to do because the evidence is not yet available."

"Being an accountant though, he may well have

some figures to support his claim."

"He may indeed, and I think if you have worked through the process with him, that we've just worked through, I would very much suspect that any evidence he had generated would be highly questionable."

"I like these skills very much, if a little concerned that they could appear to be quite aggressive in nature?"

"Yes they could be, but only if you proceed with an aggressive intention. By always pacing your colleague first and ensuring your questions are elegantly rather than aggressively delivered, then you will not come across as aggressive."

"I like the idea of elegantly delivered questions. It has a good ring to it."

"So, if we take another example, say, Mark Adams challenges your proposed changes where he said.. 'It's just too big a change. It could never work.' I think you will be able to spot some quite obvious deletions, generalisations and distortions."

"Will I take them one by one as I see them?"

"That's perfect. Fire away!"

"Well, 'It's' a simple deletion, 'too big' is a 'comparative deletion.' 'It' is another simple deletion, and, 'It could never work' is a mind read."

"Excellent! And before looking at how you could respond to this type of challenge, we also have an example of generalisations. 'Never' which did appear in a previous example we used, is what's called a 'universal quantifier' and 'could never work' is a 'modal operator of impossibility'."

"Wow, we're really hitting the jargon now!"

"Yes, unfortunately some of the terms appear jargonisitic, and once you understand them, you will recognise the significance of the terms used."

"What an elegant response to my observation." Douglas noticed how she had skilfully paced his response, and responded to it in a non-aggressive, non-defensive manner.

"I'm glad you noticed. I have to be on my toes now that you recognise and understand this area of work more clearly."

"I'll be on your case if you're not!" Douglas laughed as he pointed his finger in mock aggression. "So are you going to explain what the jargon means then?"

"Right away sir. You are becoming demanding!"

"Just keen to learn!"

They were both enjoying the fun of working together.

"'Never' is similar in nature to other words like 'always', 'everyone,' 'no-one,' 'anything' and so on. They are all-consuming as in 'never' meaning 'not ever' or 'always' meaning on every single occasion. That's why they are called 'universal quantifiers' – they quantify things in a universal way."

"Your diagnosis is working well! And how do we deal with these?"

"We basically challenge, in an elegant way of course, the generality of the word. So you could say something like… 'and, do you really mean it could never work?' with a stronger emphasis on the word never."

"Or… 'does everyone really agree with this?' in response to someone who says… 'I think everyone would agree with this point of view?'"

"Yes, that's it exactly."

"Strikes me the words 'never' and 'always' are the basis of many an argument within a relationship where one party will say ... 'you never do.. whatever' and the other party will respond with something like… 'that's all very well but you're always…' and so on."

"That'll be the argument which really turns out to be about nothing really important?"

"That's the one! So what's the other pattern you referred to as a 'modal operator' of impossibility?"

"A 'modal operator' simply refers to the mode in which a person is operating. In this case it is 'impossibility' as opposed to 'possibility,' and what we aim to do is to subtly change the other person's mode of operating away from the impossible to the possible."

"Sounds a good idea and describes quite accurately the language pattern from Mark of… 'it could never work.' A clear statement of impossibility."

"And why do people adopt this mode of thinking and operating do you think?"

"Could be simply a lack of willingness to try something different. Too much effort perhaps, or possibly they are stuck in their least-action pathway."

"So something is stopping them from seeing how this change could work. Yes? Any ideas therefore on what question you could ask?"

"I'd want to know what's stopping them."

"And a possible question in response?"

"Well, the obvious one is to ask 'what's stopping it, or going to stop it, from working?'"

"Which is again the right response."

"So here's the whole process in response to Mark's… 'It's too big a change. It could never work.' I would firstly pace him by saying… 'I can understand that you think this its too big a change and that it could never work?'"

"A good pace. And next?"

"I would have to clarify what he means by 'it' being too big a 'change.' After that I could ask him what would stop the now clarified 'it' from working and, if necessary, what evidence he has that it won't work."

"Brilliant! He could come back to the 'too big' in relation to 'what's stopping the change from working' which you rightly didn't deal with initially and will have recognised as a 'comparative deletion.'"

"I would then ask him 'in what way is the change too big?'"

"That would work well. You could also be a bit devilish and ask what level of change would work. You're certainly getting the hang of this. Well done."

"Thanks again. I can really see how the process of understanding more clearly what lies behind the resistance and challenges people present to us can help to overcome the resistance, and assist people to see the value of a change."

"And while we're on 'modal operators,' let me introduce you to 'necessity' which often goes hand-in-hand with 'impossibility.' When you ask someone 'what's stopping you?' you will frequently get a response like 'because we need to, or have to, do it this way.'"

"So they are once again demonstrating their least action pathway?"

"Yes, quite clearly in this instance."

"And the response?"

"The response has to challenge their current attachment to necessity in a particular case. It needs to help to blow a hole in this 'necessity.' We want them to have to create a different scenario in their minds, so we ask them... 'what would happen if you didn't do it this way?'"

"Yes, I can see how that would work because if it was me being asked that question, I would have to think through what an alternative scenario could look like."

"There are variations and developments in this case and I think this will be sufficient for you at the moment except for one last addition to dealing with impossibility which I forgot earlier. Once we have ascertained 'what's stopping them?' which is almost in one hundred percent of cases, themselves, we can then ask 'and what could you/we do to make it work effectively?'"

"Bringing 'collective responsibility' nicely back into the frame."

"A good point especially by using 'we' rather than 'you.' How do you feel now about handling resistance to change or challenges to the changes you want to make?"

"Much more confident than I would have been without these new skills, although aware that I have still much to learn and that I will require to practice the skills as often as possible. So, if I had to deal with Stewart's other comment where he says...'if these changes don't work' I can immediately spot a modal operator of impossibility at work and would ask, in an elegant manner, of course, what would stop the changes from working in the first place. I still have the underlying confidence that I will be able to implement the changes that I want and create a culture of collective responsibility through 'Our Business' concept, and believe that these new developing skills will help me do so more smoothly and more swiftly."

"And just to remind you that we did come across

another distortion earlier in our discussion. Remember?"

"That was around the concept of a 'meeting' being abstract rather than a tangible object."

"That's the one!"

'What was that called again? Something around nominal I seem to remember."

"Pretty close actually. It's a nominalization. In classic NLP they will say if you can't put it in a wheelbarrow, it's a nominalization. One of the classics is the term 'communication.' You will constantly hear people complaining about 'poor communication', or that we need to improve our 'communication.'"

"Very non-specific?"

"And it means pretty much what you want it to mean."

"So how do we go about 'recovering' the nominalization?"

"Well, most nominalizations are actually verbs that have been turned into a noun, so the way to 'recover' it is to turn it back into a verb. So how would you respond to the comment about improving communication?"

"Something around ...'in what ways do you want me/us to communicate more effectively.'"

"Good. By turning the noun into a verb, we can now be very specific about what we want to improve. Another classic is 'confrontation.' When the verb to confront is turned into the noun 'confrontation' it takes on a whole new meaning."

"I can see now that it's very productive to 'confront' a difficult issue, and yet when turned into the noun 'confrontation', people may avoid dealing with the issue because of the connotations which the word places on it?"

"Yes, exactly. They confuse the word confront with the term conflict. To confront someone doesn't mean experiencing conflict, whereas a confrontation almost assumes conflict."

"We could go on further if you want. Are you happy with what we've done?"

"Very happy, Lise. As always – and yes, I do mean always – you have brought to life, in your own inimitable style, a subject area that could otherwise be quite challenging to grasp. All that's left for me now is to stay conscious enough to put the skills into practice."

"Ah, and I forgot to tell you. That scenario we experienced was only an example of what could happen in the future, depending of course on how skilfully the change process is managed." Lise informed Douglas in deadpan style.

Douglas nodded and smiled in appreciation at how Lise had created the circumstances for real learning to take place.

Chapter Fifteen

Reflections

"The complacent company is a dead company. Success today requires the agility and drive to constantly rethink, reinvigorate, react and reinvent."

Bill Gates

After Lise left his office, Douglas spent a couple of hours reading and responding to emails and ensuring that he was up-to-date with his work schedule. He always felt re-invigorated after working with Lise. He felt sharper, more focused and inspired to face the challenges that lay ahead. His thoughts turned once again to his vision of the future for 'Silver Waters,' a future that he had once envisaged for 'Guardian Angel.' And yet he realised that 'Guardian Angel' had been a stepping-stone to his present circumstances and that without the upheaval experienced by his move, he would have been unlikely to have acquired the level of insight which he now possessed. His adventures in Peru, and his continuation of his work with Lise had further opened his mind and heart to the possibilities of creating and sustaining a business where the culture and climate generated the energy, vision, innovation and commitment to make it a place where people would want to work. And, of course, generate the levels of excellence and success from which everyone could benefit. 'Is it really possible?' he had asked the same question of himself so many times. He considered himself an optimist, and still, at his age, an idealist. But he also considered himself a realist, so he had to find practical ways to achieve his ideals, his vision. He knew he would be shot down in flames if all he came up with were concepts. Yes, he needed the concepts as starting points, and yes, he would want people to understand these concepts. And, the crucial element was whether people could see tangible changes that in time would benefit them all.

And, of course, he knew that opposition and resistance to his ideas lay ahead in the future, just in the same way that bunkers lie ahead for the golfer as they set out on the first of eighteen holes, and for professionals in competitions, seventy two holes. He knew that, using the golfing analogy, that amateur golfers usually cursed their bad luck if they landed in a bunker; perhaps also cursing the weather, the golf-course architect and anyone else they could think of – especially if they land in a footprint which some previous player had failed to rake over. In this state of mind, they invariably fluff their shot, remaining in the bunker or only just managing to escape from it. Contrast this, thought Douglas, with the professionals approach. They understand and appreciate that bunkers are part of the course, part of the game of golf. They obviously don't aim to land in them, but because they know they are out there, they have prepared themselves for that eventuality. They practice the skills necessary to get out, if possible without losing any shots. Douglas can remember

Peter Allis, the legendary golf commentator explaining to his television audience in hushed tones – as if he were standing close-by instead of being tucked up in the BBC Commentary box – that the player who had hit his shot and landed at the side of the green, behind and outside the bunker which lay there, would rather have been in the bunker! 'Heaven forbid!' Douglas could hear legions of amateur golfers crying out. And yet, if they had though about it, they would understand that the professional doesn't simply practice the 'easy' shots. Or stand on a driving range and hit drives for a couple of hours. They spend time ensuring they can get out of any trouble they get into too. So, if their ball lands in a green side bunker they know they have the skill to not only get it out, but also get it close enough to the hole to ensure they don't drop any shots to par. His previous session with Lise had been in effect a lesson in 'bunker shots.' Not only being aware of the challenges that lay ahead, but also practicing the skills to overcome these challenges – the 'Bunkers' – which he and his colleagues could face and move through smoothly.

He knew that he had to get his immediate team onside. He had to allay their fears that may exist in a period of change and he had to create a climate of real openness where doubts and fears could be raised and dealt with together.

He wanted his team to be confident in taking risks, and helping to build that confidence through developing their 'bunker' skills. He realised that he could not do this on his own, and although he also realised that his colleagues could not replicate his own unique process of development, he had to provide them with the opportunities for developing the skills needed to take the business forward. This could be in their capacity as a leader or manager, as a team coach, as a strategist, as a team player. It could relate to their technical skills or to their resilience under pressure. He was particularly keen that they would be at the cutting edge in all elements of business and would ensure that their technology allowed them to be at the forefront of their market, able to deliver outstanding service throughout their customer portfolio.

He wanted to take 'Silver Waters' from its current boutique status, to be seen to be a respected player in the global market. Not big enough to attract yet another take-over bid, but big enough to have enough clout in the market place. To be able to attract and pay the top people available and to ensure the year-on-year growth required to sustain the confidence of their clients, their investors, and of course, inevitably, the city.

Chapter Sixteen

Another "Journey"

"The Great man is he who does not lose his child's heart"
Mencius c371 – c291 BC

"Welcome back my friend!" Sam was standing in front of him, all teeth and sparkling eyes. "How was your journey?"

"Very similar to my previous one except I was more in the flow than before and simply allowed the water to bring me here." Douglas was slightly out of breath, as his journey on what had felt again like a water cushion, had seemed longer than before. As if he had travelled deeper down into the cavern.

"It's great to see you again!" Sam stepped forward and gave him his customary hug. "And how has life been for you since we last met?"

"Amazing Sam, just amazing! You probably won't believe this, but I've been to your native country since we last met." Douglas had disengaged himself from Sam but still stood close enough to be able to put his right hand on Sam's shoulder.

"Oh, I believe it!" Sam's laughter reverberated around the underground cavern. "I have inside information you know!"

"I thought you might. You had that look on your face."

"It's my job you know, to keep tabs on you."

"Thanks Sam, I appreciate that. And what have you got in store for me today?"

"You may remember that we didn't finish our journey the last time you were here."

"I do indeed. I think you said there were four chambers to visit. Is that correct?"

"Well remembered! Yes, on your first journey here we visited the chambers of organisational Wounds and Contracts."

Douglas nodded in agreement.

"And on this visit we will explore the Chamber of your Passions and the Chamber of Gifts."

"Sounds less traumatic than my previous visit?"

"Indeed, I think it most certainly will be. And I believe you have done some good work around your first experience here."

Douglas nodded in agreement. "And I have the most challenging work left ahead of me. Putting our concepts and philosophies into action."

"You will do it my friend, you will do it. Our work together will confirm that you are aligned to your own true path, your own true purpose." Sam placed his hand between Douglas's shoulder blades and indicated they were ready to move on.

Douglas was once again intrigued. He had spent some time contemplating what his true purpose in life was, and had felt that his decision to leave 'Guardian Angel' when he did reflected that he had become aware that he was here in this lifetime to achieve more than the material benefits that were available to him if he had stayed. Nothing ventured, he thought, as he moved forward under Sam's guidance.

The cavern seemed to Douglas to be lighter than before, helped he reckoned, by the lit torches which burned brightly along the path which they were walking. He certainly felt less fearful than he had on his first journey here, uplifted almost. And this time he realised that although his first experience with Sam had been a dream, this experience – as with the last – felt so real. He pondered on Thomas Wolfe's quote about dreams and reality and felt a shiver of excitement run through his body.

"This way," Sam veered across a small stone bridge and into a flagstone path, "Almost there." he turned and grinned at Douglas, nodding his head as if to confirm that the experience which lay ahead would be inspiring and fulfilling for Douglas.

"Wow!" Douglas couldn't believe it. They had, initially entered an enclosed walk-way which was adorned with beautiful climbing plants, like clematis he thought, growing on each side, meeting above them on the roof of the walkway in a mass of bloom. Purple, white, pinks and reds mingled to produce a spectacular display of both colour and scents. They had to crouch forward a little to avoid the blooms before entering what reminded Douglas so much of Peru.

"What a fabulous place, so this is the Chamber of Passions? Is that what you said?"

"It is indeed. The Chamber of your Passions!"

"So what does that mean exactly?"

"It means that here you will find, or perhaps, confirm what your passions are in your life, what really motivates you."

"Does this relate to my life's purpose?"

"It's all tied up together. You've made a number of key decisions in your life of late that in their own way demonstrate what your purpose is. I hope you like what this has in store for you." Sam indicated to Douglas to follow him down a fairly steep path that took them on to a grassy terrace overlooking a broad fast running river. The river threaded its way through lush green valleys and meadows transforming firstly into a series of terraces and then spectacularly into snow capped mountains. Sam signalled for Douglas to sit down at the edge of the terrace where they were able to look up and down river. Up-river the terrain was more mountainous, whereas down river it opened out into cultivated valleys with small houses and hamlets dotted across the landscape.

"This is magnificent." Douglas had that marvellous sense of connection with his surroundings once again that he had experienced in Peru. That wonderful energy that pulsated from the mountains, and this amazing natural space. Douglas had always treasured his walks by the river close to his house with his dog, Tara. The motion and sound of water had regularly both calmed him and inspired him over the years. In recent times with his work with Lise, his reading experiences and new found awareness, he found the flow of water to be as a marvellous metaphor for life. Rivers have no doubts or fears about moving forward. No 'will I,' 'won't I,' 'should I,' 'shouldn't I.' They simply flow, and move on towards the mouth of the river. They reminded him to 'get himself out of his own way" and to let himself flow. He had caught a piece on the television recently where Tiger Woods was explaining this experience of 'getting in the flow'. He had said that when he was playing at his peak – which in Douglas's mind was all the time! – he 'got himself out of the way' as if he was detached from himself. Almost as if he was watching himself play. In this place there were no doubts, fears or anxiety. He was able to release his true potential and play his best golf.

And this was no ordinary river Sam and he were watching. It's power and majesty was immense. It's roar almost deafening as it pounded over and around its rocky edges towards its ultimate destination.

"Just sit and listen," Sam whispered "without attachment to thought." Douglas breathed easily and listened.

"What do you think?" Sam asked, after what seemed like about ten minutes.

"Difficult to explain," replied Douglas. "This whole experience I find uplifting and energising."

"And you won't be surprised then that this is the first part of your passion?"

"Do you mean Peru, or rivers or what?"

"Your connection with natural spaces. The whole experience. It brings out the best in you; opens your mind to the possibilities in life."

Douglas had often experienced great connections in natural spaces but only since his trip to Peru had he realised how significant these experiences were to his life.

He nodded in agreement.

Douglas had realised the importance of natural spaces in the workplace, using plants, trees and water to assist the well-being, health and efficiency of his colleagues at Silver Waters. He loved the company name and had already made plans to incorporate, where possible, water features within the office. He had also employed designers who specialised in using natural substances like stone, wood, slate, glass etc, to create an internal/external environment that energised rather than de-energised his people. Plans were also afoot to acquire or build an out of town learning and development centre for the business.

"Shall we move on?" Sam standing up and indicated that they moved down river towards the populated areas.

As he walked, Douglas was aware of his feet in the ground, feeling the weight of his body with each step on the lush grassy terrace on which they walked. And at the same time he felt a lightness within himself – filled with sami or refined energy, as the Andeans would call it. Their path took them gradually downwards towards the valley and to the hamlets they had viewed from the terrace where they set out. As they walked without talking, with only the roar of the river, occasional bird song and the rustle of grasses in the light breeze as background company, Douglas became aware that they were now also being accompanied by a variety of gorgeous butterflies. They seemed particularly attracted to Douglas as they fluttered around his head and occasionally landing briefly on his shoulder.

"Let's take a seat." Sam pointed to two large flat stones that seemed conveniently placed for them to sit down on.

As they sat down, the butterflies continued their performance for Douglas, reminding him of his experiences in the Peruvian jungle several months ago. He had become more conscious even at home of butterflies and how they had appeared on his walks as he chewed over a difficult decision.

"Beautiful, aren't they?" Douglas turned to Sam as one of the butterflies landed gently on the back of his hand.

"And a symbol of another of your passions." Sam laughed as one of them landed on top of Douglas's head.

"Of wild life?"

"Not exactly." Sam was amused at Douglas's sense of humour. "Butterflies are symbols of change, of transformation. They represent your passion for personal growth and transformation."

Douglas had only really awakened to the possibilities of real growth through his association with Lise, although up to that time he had had a nagging feeling that there was something more, something that he hadn't yet accessed. Hence, he thought, I had pursued a number of potential development paths through traditional business routes, before his journey with Lise opened his eyes and his mind to real personal growth.

"I can thank Lise for awakening me to this, and yes, it is most definitely a continuing passion for me. And I can see the close links between these two passions, in that my experiences in natural spaces has helped me to open my transformational energy and has helped support me through the challenges that this brings with it."

This he had begun to realise was what many people failed to recognise when they seek personal change and growth. That the challenges become bigger, rather than smaller. Many people are seeking something which doesn't exist, a life without problems or challenges. What he was now beginning to understand about himself was that he needed the energy he got from places like this, to sustain him through the changes which he intended to implement in 'Silver Waters,' and, of course in his own life. And equally he realised the importance of this interdependence for the changes he wanted to implement at 'Silver Waters.'

"It's a beautiful calming experience sitting here

with these wonderful creatures surrounding me breathing in this pure fresh air and feeling the heat of the morning sun across the back of my shoulders." Douglas took a deep breath and soaked in his surroundings once more, as Sam stood up with the indication that they were on the move again. They strolled further through the valley, again allowing nature to provide the conversation. They were heading slowly towards a small hamlet that they had spotted earlier. As they reached its outskirts, Douglas recognised it as similar to a number he had come across when in Peru. It had one main street that threaded its way past a hotchpotch of quite primitively built houses. The road, of course, was unmettled, and at present was a hard and dusty dirt track. In the rainy season, Douglas imagined it would be most unpleasant. They were greeted a hundred metres or so from the first houses by a small group of children who seemed delighted to see them, and accompanied them towards the village. As they walked down the main street they could see that at the end of the village there was a market that seemed out of proportion to the size of the village.

"This is a weekly market where people from surrounding areas bring their wares to sell or barter, whichever way works for them." Sam led Douglas through the bustling market where everyone attempted to attract their attention to stop and buy their goods. There was local jewellery, fabrics, clothes, meat, fruit and vegetables, the usual range of items that Douglas had seen on his Peruvian travels. Occasionally they would be surrounded by smiling children looking to sell them cards and trinkets. The energy of the people seemed to match the energy of their environment, Douglas thought. There were no glum faces, no one trying to outdo or outsell their neighbours. The sense of community was obvious. The spirit of Ayni, of reciprocity, was self evident, the basis of Andean life. These people lived with the awareness that without the spirit of reciprocity their lives would be even harder than they were. By truly living and working as a community, they were able to survive in often very difficult circumstances.

Sam looked quizzically at Douglas, as if to say 'so what do you take from this?'

"The sense of energy and community from the people. Their willingness to work together and where possible, embrace any changes which will improve the quality of their community."

"Yes, your third and final passion. People and Community."

"Which is just as well considering my job and the challenges I've set up for myself."

"Ah, indeed." Sam looked thoughtful, for once not demonstrating his spectacular smile. "But there are many people who hold positions such as yours who have no real concern for people or community."

Spot on thought Douglas. This really had been his battle ever since he began to implement the changes at 'Guardian Angel.' Persuading his peers that it was possible not only to generate financial success, but also to create a sense of involvement and community within the workplace.

"I know." replied Douglas. "Makes for exciting challenges ahead."

"You like your Passions then?" Sam began to guide Douglas beyond the market and the edge of the village towards a rocky outcrop about fifty metres ahead. "Couldn't be better. Each one complements the other and together they provide a richness and roundedness to my life."

"People, natural places and growth. Your three passions to support your life's purpose."

Douglas nodded in agreement. He probably couldn't previously have articulated exactly what they were but, felt a real congruence across the three. He loved natural spaces; he was committed to his own personal growth and was fascinated by the challenge of creating an organisation that could claim to be a success for all who were involved. They had reached the rocky outcrop to which they had been heading.

"I'll go first." Sam said ducking down slightly to get himself through. Douglas could see this was the entry to another new space. Douglas had to bend down much further than Sam, being almost a foot taller.

"Gosh! Not what I expected!" Douglas exclaimed as he straightened himself up and took in his new surroundings. A small outdoor amphitheatre with a giant screen opposite man-made grassy terraced seats. It reminded him of an unused but still evident outdoor 'theatre' he had come across once in Braidburn Valley Park in Edinburgh.

"What's today's main feature then?" he joked with Sam.

"The life and times of that well known Scottish superstar, Douglas Murray. Or at least I should say the recent life and times. We haven't got all day you know." Sam was beaming again.

"Or night for that matter!"

"Touché my friend! Now sit back and have a look at what we have in store for you."

Sam nodded in the direction of the giant screen,

which, as if obeying his command, lit itself up with Douglas's face beaming back at them in glorious Technicolor. Douglas, for the first time in a while, felt vaguely uncomfortable, not knowing what was in store for him.

"Let's role!" Sam shouted.

As Douglas's face faded out, it was replaced with a scene in his old office at 'Guardian Angel' – it was a rerun of his first meeting with Lise. Douglas sat back feeling more relaxed and curious now. "So, it's the life and times of the new Douglas Murray?" Douglas slapped Sam gently between his shoulder blades.

Sam nodded in agreement.

As this first scenario faded, another along his 'journey' with Lise appeared. There was the episode in the football dressing room, his experience in the wood where they left the 'well trodden path,' his numerous adventures when he was able to sit in on colleague meetings whilst remaining invisible. Wow! Did he remember the impact these insights had had on him! And then there was the runaway carriage. Now that was frightening, but it had the effect of helping him understand his relationship with his ego.

Also showing were many frustrating meetings where he had to work hard to persuade his colleagues of the benefits of, the changes he proposed. And yes, there was the reserved parking spaces for senior managers – one of the changes he had baulked at- and the exclusive lift to the seventh floor. His first morning walk through the office floors where many of his colleagues looked as if they had seen a ghost when he appeared. There were, of course, the sessions where Lise was able to show him the consequences of his and his colleague's actions. And culminating in his lone fight to keep 'Guardian

Angel' independent and the subsequent takeover by Universal Bank Inc.

Then there were the more 'recent' events – his experiences in Peru, and his first dream where he journeyed through the Chambers of Organisational Wounds and Contracts and the subsequent creation of new, more productive contracts to help him transform his new business. There was his meeting with his new colleagues and his lengthy session with Lise on pacing and the Meta Model which had strengthened his confidence in handling resistance to change or challenges to new ideas.

After reviewing what he had just experienced with Sam, Lise appeared magically on the screen to 'Round Off' his journey.

"Your major challenges still lie ahead." she began. Douglas's stomach tightened at the prospect, but was committed to viewing what may lie ahead with a positive attitude and a clear intention to succeed.

"No, we have no footage of what is in store for you. You will be the architect and creator of the journey as you have been to date, using your new-found awareness and skills to generate the outcomes and success you desire and have envisaged."

"To help you and your colleagues on the way, we have provided you with three 'gifts' to take with you. Three qualities that you yourself have been developing along the way and which also may be needed by your close colleagues and allies in your quest to create the type of 'connected' company that you want."

Douglas had no idea what these 'gifts' would be but had complete faith in Lise's judgement to know that they would be what he required.

"Patience is your first gift. You will need large

quantities of this as you pursue your dream."

Douglas nodded, knowing that he hadn't always been the most patient person in the world. He recalled one of his favourite phrases that he had used frequently in the past, that he 'didn't suffer fools gladly' now realising the disrespect that this bestowed on his fellow human beings.

"Resilience is your next gift and matches nicely with patience. You will need to stay strong in the face of significant resistance. I know this is a quality which you have already developed powerfully over the years."

Douglas again nodded, this time in thanks.

"You will also require to assist your colleagues to develop their own resilience, to follow through with the changes that you want them to implement."

Douglas realised the challenge and equally felt that he was well prepared for it.

"And finally, the gift of intuition, of your intuitive sense, which you have been opening up to since we started working together. This will be an essential element in making the correct decisions on the challenging journey that lies ahead. Blending the rational / logical with your intuitive self will provide you with the perfect means to navigate yourself and your business through any rough seas along the way."

'And encouraging others to open up to their own intuitive self also, will be essential.' Douglas thought to himself.

"Bon Voyage!"…

… And Lise disappeared from the screen.

"Well!" Sam stood up and turned to Douglas with his arms out stretched.

"Hasta Luego, my dear friend."

"Hasta Luego indeed!" Douglas replied after they had completed their farewell hug. Sam flashed one last tooth-filled smile, turned and quickly disappeared into a nearby rocky outcrop.

"Hasta Luego, Hasta Luego!" Douglas repeated louder as Sam disappeared.

"Aren't you going to dress before leaving?"

Pat was gently shaking him awake. Douglas turned round slowly and smiled at her, not quite back from his so-conscious dream.

"Wow!" was all he could say before taking a deep breath and sitting up with his back, and head supported by the headboard.

"Another interesting one?" Pat asked.

"It was Sam again. A continuation from the last one, and once again so real. It felt truly as if I was actually with him."

"Why don't I go and make some tea and you can talk it through with me?"

"A great idea!" Douglas was already scribbling notes on the pad he always kept beside his bed. "I need to write it down to ensure I can take full benefit from the experience."

"Hasta Luego then Mr Dreamer!" Pat disappeared out of the bedroom on her way downstairs to the kitchen.

"And so to work..." Douglas whispered to himself.

Chapter Seventeen

Fulfilling the Dream

"When we dream alone, it is only a dream. When we dream together, it is no longer a dream but the beginning of reality."

Brazilian Proverb

Douglas strolled along side the river on his favourite walk, his consciousness of the beneficial effect of this experience heightened through his journeys in Peru. Since his first trip, he had been there on another two occasions, the first time with Pat and the second on his own. Pat had had some difficulty with the altitude and was happy to have Douglas travel without her on his next trip. He had been pleased in many ways to have the opportunity to explore his favourite country on his own, meeting up with some of the friends he had made on previous occasions. The chance to do his 'own thing.' Now that he had retired from his position at 'Silver Waters' after five very successful – and challenging years – he planned to continue his exploration of Peru and other South American Countries.

Tara, his constant companion on these walks these

past twelve years, was still by his side. He had noticed just lately she was showing signs of age, a bit like himself he thought – getting a bit stiff around the joints. Not so stiff that stopped him working out and playing golf, or stopped Tara from chasing a stick or seeing off the neighbour's cat if it ventured into her domain.

"Five years since I left 'Guardian Angel,'" Douglas was in reflective mood. Normally never one to look back, Douglas couldn't help wondering … 'what if?' What if he had stayed on? What if it hadn't been sold? What if he had never met Lise? So much pain in extracting himself from the business to which he had dedicated most of his working life. Preparing him for what came next was how he viewed it now. Although Douglas could come across outwardly as pretty tough and strong, he had never enjoyed 'endings' as he called them. The end of a relationship, the end of someone's life, the end of a job or project, even the end of a great holiday. He had always felt a level of some sadness at these moments, shedding a tear only when alone and out of sight. And now he had come to the end of his relationship with 'Silver Waters'. He had always had it in his mind to give it five years at most. Enough time to achieve what he wanted, and to prepare the ground, most importantly for his people to build on what he had helped to put in place.

He had been jotting down some notes of what he felt he had achieved over the past five years. Notes that would form the basis of a report to the board, and perhaps even a book at some time in the future.

"Not sure if anyone would want to read It." he had said to Pat that morning, "but it would be fun to write I think." She had nodded to him with that knowing look on her face. Knowing that once an idea had formed in his mind, Douglas would almost always follow through with it. So a "perhaps a book" would most certainly mean he already had some of his ideas mapped out.

And she wasn't wrong. His notes had been structured so as to enable him to create a story out of the list of challenges, achievements, outcomes, initiatives, and all the activities he had been involved in over the years, including those at 'Guardian Angel.' And he knew that several publishers were interested.

"Oh boy!" he laughed to himself as he pictured some of his old colleagues reading an account of his exploits with Lise – the meetings he had sat in on without their knowledge. The invisible CEO would take on a whole new meaning!

He focused for the moment on his past five years at 'Silver Waters' sitting down on his favourite stone where he had wrestled with many conundrums over the years. Tara settled herself down in front of him, head on paws, her eyes half shut, half open, just in case he decided to move on.

'What had he achieved?' was how he had tackled it. He wanted the details of this to be presented to emphasise that the innovations that he had both initiated and stimulated in others, had produced tangible, and in many cases, measurable outcomes and benefits.

He wasn't indicating that he had personally come up with every new idea, more that he had created a climate in which people were stimulated to generate innovations, where they were confident that they would at least be heard and listened to.

He flicked over the cover of his notes. First in line were business results that he had lain out in percentage terms comparing them from his starting point five years previously.

He checked the figures.

Average Annual Sales Increase	37%
Assets Under Management Increased from	25bn to 120bn
Average Annual New Business Margin Over 5 Years	34.6%

He nodded in satisfaction at the progress the business had made under his stewardship. Most importantly, they had consistently outperformed and surpassed their competitors over his five years in charge. The key, he knew, had been both in the people he had recruited and retained and in the development of those people he had inherited. Responses to job adverts always resulted in a deluge of applications, although many appointments were made on recommendations from current members of the team. Douglas and his colleagues had also always been on the lookout for best practice ideas and innovations in other businesses. So not every idea was unique to themselves; what was unique was the overall package built on Douglas's concept of 'Our Business,' which was next up in his draft report...

He had introduced and implemented the 'Our Business' Culture within his first twelve months in post. He had taken his management team away to a five star venue for a long weekend – inviting partners to join them for dinner and overnight stay on the Saturday – and worked through the elements of the culture and how it could be best implemented, with the help of a skilled facilitator – he would have liked to involve Lise but thought it may not be appropriate –they refined the 'contracts,' the 'values,' and 'rewards,' including measurement of performance.

He emphasised his belief in the philosophies, passed onto him by the Andeans in Peru, of Anyi – or reciprocity – and Munay – or love from the heart – rather than operating through a culture of fear and blame which seemed to be prevalent across many organisations across the private, public and not-for-profit sectors. Learning from his initial insights at 'Guardian Angel' with Lise, he reinforced their understanding of their key role in making a success of the new culture. Their behaviour including of course, his own, would be crucial in sending a signal out to the rest of the business about the way it would be run. They would all make mistakes of course, and had to be prepared to support rather than point the finger at their colleagues.

By the end of the weekend they had agreements on the content of the changes and crucially, on how they would be implemented. He wanted each of them, as well as himself, to be involved in cascading the culture throughout the business. They would probably require some input from outside the business. But being seen to take ownership of the culture themselves, they agreed, was vital to its success. They didn't want the process to be dull and uninteresting. They wanted to create a lively, participative process to engage all their colleagues, and with tangible relevant elements for all concerned.

One approach that Douglas wanted to develop was that of 'story telling' particularly in relation to the 'Silver Waters' story. He had read a good deal about its benefits within organisations as a means of promoting change. The current organisational story telling guru appeared to be Stephen Denning, formerly Programme Director for Knowledge Management at the World Bank. Douglas and his team, with the help of their facilitator, had laid the foundations for their 'story'. This would be used in the cascading process, encouraging all involved to contribute to its development, and subsequently as part of inductions. It would also be updated annually and used as an innovative way of agreeing and communicating the annual goals for each coming year. This was something that had worked really well over the years and had stimulated great bursts of creativity as people became personally involved. The 'Silver Waters Story' was now part of the folklore of the business and colleagues across the business had become engaging storytellers who were involved in induction programmes, workshops and business PR events.

One of the key outcomes from the initial weekend was an agreement on the language that they would use to sell the new culture. There would be no 'ifs,' 'trys' or 'mights,' only 'when,' 'do' and 'will.' They all understood the significance of using productive language and agreed to help coach each other if any of them slipped back. Douglas also wanted to change the language within the business. He wanted 'Silver Waters' referred to as the 'Business' rather than 'Company' which was one of many military terms he had begun to notice were used in organisations. 'Staff' would be 'colleagues' and 'departments' and 'units' etc would become 'teams.' He also disliked the idea of having a team called 'Human Resources' and had floated the idea of renaming it the 'People Team.'

Peter Fisher, his HR Director had looked as if he'd seen a ghost when Douglas had suggested this. His mouth was moving but nothing came out! Douglas chuckled to himself as he recalled the scene. Tara opened an eye to check that all was well with her master.

After his initial opposition, Peter had agreed to make the change helped by some good-natured ribbing from his colleagues. Douglas had often looked back on these four days they had spent together as one of the most significant events of his working life. It had given him the chance to communicate his dreams and desires and excitement of the possibilities that lay ahead. It also created a bond with his team that had not just been sustained, but had been strengthened over the years. He had also made a point of having at least two team development events each year and on the occasions when there had been additions or changes to the team, they had added an extra event to help to integrate the new colleague quickly into the workings of the team.

One of their key tangible planks for building 'Our Business' was a share options scheme, whereby after twelve months, everyone was given the same initial package. Future awards were made in relation to the significance of their contribution to the business and not their position in the business. Further packages were offered to colleagues to buy at preferential rates. This had been hugely positive across the business. Not a new idea he realised, but its popularity, Douglas felt, had been broadly due to the culture in which it operated. People really did feel it was 'Their Business,' and very few people cashed in their options while still employed within the business.

Overall, the cascading process had been successful. He had personally welcomed each colleague group who were involved and had lunch with them on Day One and had drinks with them at the end of the workshop. The process had not been without its challenges with resistance coming through on a few occasions. These had been used as live examples on which to base their conflict resolution programme. Looking back, Douglas could see the power of the saying that…"The People Who Challenge Us Most Are Our Best Teachers." The 'Conflict Resolution' Programme had now become compulsory for all colleagues to take. Handling disagreements and conflict using Adult state behaviour rather than wasting energy and focus resorting to Child state behaviours, had released a huge amount of energy and increased overall levels of productivity. They had employed an outside company to help them with this aspect of behaviour, hence his knowledge – only a little he realised – of Transactional Analysis and the use of terms like Adult and Child state behaviour. He had also realised how much Parent behaviour he had used in the past…

"Not now though?" he asked Tara. She opened both eyes this time and looked at him as if to say "Aye that'll be right!"

Rewards had been, as always, one of the trickiest elements of any business. Money had been shown, through numerous pieces of research over many years, not to be a prime motivator in the workplace. Rather, it had been shown to be a potential de-motivator. This meant, as Douglas had understood it to mean, that more money didn't make an individual's job better, or increase the motivation of someone on the job, it just meant they didn't moan about not having enough money. Money was a symbol, particularly in relation to how much people felt valued. Although Douglas was well aware that, if people were disaffected with an organisation, more money would seldom repair their distrust or disillusionment. Very much like a relationship, Douglas mused. When two people are truly in love, or are in the first stage of romantic love, even the smallest gift is received with massive appreciation and feelings of mutual affection. On the other hand, when a relationship is on the rocks, and disillusionment has set in, not even the most expensive gift will have an effect. The lesson, he had realised, was to create a business and business culture, where people enjoyed working and from which they were able to extract some of their psychic income as well as financial gain. There were, of course, age-old issues like equality, longevity etc. where people compared themselves against their colleagues. Through 'Our Business,' Douglas and his team had set out to overcome any dissatisfaction people may have around their financial package. They had looked at the factors of seniority, contribution to business success, and length of service, and had been very open and transparent about the workings of the process.

Peter Fisher was the known expert in this field and had been actively involved in a number of major research projects over the years. And, he had a very talented team working with him. He had introduced a goal of creating and offering what is known as a Flexible Benefits Package. Quoting from the CIPD*(The Chartered Institute of Personnel and Development) website.

Peter explained that Flexible Benefits Schemes… "are formalised systems that allow employees to vary their pay and benefits package in order to satisfy their personal requirements." "With these schemes," he

---

*Full details can be found on the CIPD website www.cipd.co.uk

had continued, "the dividing line between pay and benefits becomes less rigid than in standard reward packages." He had also indicated that although historically these had been difficult schemes to manage, he had investigated new software that would make this much easier.

It was definitely the type of approach that Douglas favoured, and after some discussion to clarify certain issues, they tasked Peter to set up the programme. The scheme had turned out to be very popular with the workforce and reckoned to be a contributing factor for their very low people turnover.

They had initially offered the following benefits in the scheme to all their colleagues, not necessarily all at the time of employment:

- Pension
- Life Insurance
- Private Medical Insurance and Alternative Health Treatments
- Child Care Vouchers
- Car Scheme
- Bike Purchase and Hire Schemes
- Retail Vouchers
- Travel / Holiday vouchers

And over the first two years of the scheme they added:

- Increased Holiday Entitlement
- Dental care Insurance
- Critical Illness Insurance
- Personal Accident Insurance
- Personal Coaching

Douglas looked back now with pride at how effective the scheme had been, and how they had encouraged people to become truly involved. A number of the above elements had been expanded and developed as a result of input from his colleagues across all areas of the business.

Douglas made a few notes beside this section of his report and turned over to the next page.

"Ah! Personal and Career Development." he said out loud, stirring Tara very briefly. "An area close to my heart." he thought. He reviewed this section with pride as he believed they had created some truly innovative development routes for their colleagues to follow. Douglas had wrestled for a number of years with the way in which individuals could make progress within a business. Traditionally i.e. in organisations – the only route was to become a manager, or supervisor, of other people. Unfortunately, he had seen many examples of talented people foundering on the rocks of people management. Many tried to carry on doing what they had been good at before they were promoted and frustrating the hell out of their colleagues who reported to them. Others simply avoided dealing with people issues, unable to confront any challenges from colleagues, and allowed mistrust, communication breakdowns etc. to fester. Whatever form it manifested, Douglas had come to realise that not everyone who was a talented technician – i.e. accountant, teacher etc., would be a talented manager. Yet societal financial and peer group pressures often forced people to accept these posts.

What he and his colleagues had introduced was two basic routes to personal advancement. The 'traditional' or 'vertical' route through the various tiers of management, and a 'horizontal' route, which included what Douglas liked to call the 'Professorial' route. Taking this route, an individual would be given opportunities to expand their current skills further and become an acknowledged 'expert' in their field – someone to whom individuals and the business looked for information, innovations, and a deeper knowledge of their field than the norm. Another option on the 'horizontal route' was the opportunity to become an in-house coach or a 'Silver Waters Storyteller.' It had taken a year or two for people to become comfortable about looking at this 'new' route for personal progress as a feasible alternative to the 'Managerial Route.' The fact that there were associated financial rewards included, assisted in this process. What they had very few of – if any, Douglas hoped – were managers who were square pegs in a round hole.

And of course they had developed a very comprehensive management development and coaching programme for those who chose the 'vertical' or 'managerial' route. In this respect he had been very impressed by the research carried out by Marcus Buckingham and Curt Coffman which was described in their book, 'First, Break All the Rules'. They had researched managers' performance and team culture through an extensive employee survey. And, this had been no ordinary survey. It had included 2,500 business units, 105,000 employees interviewing 80,000 managers in all. Their research had confirmed Douglas's experience that the success of individual business teams was, above all dependent on the way in which individual managers manage those teams and create productive working environments for their colleagues. He realised that it was pointless having a set of corporate values and a desired culture unless his managers were actually operating through these on a day-to-day basis.

Firstly, Buckingham and Coffman found that those

employees who had responded more positively to the twelve question survey they had developed, worked in business units with higher levels of productivity, profit, people retention and customer satisfaction. This had translated sales and profits into two key tangible outcomes. The difference in the sales performance between the top and bottom 25% in the survey had been $104 Million and those in the top 25% of the survey were 14% over their profit budget, while those in the bottom 25% missed their targets by 30%.

The survey, Douglas had been delighted to read, had not related to performance metrics or statistical analysis of products and markets or managing through bureaucratic procedures. It had focused on how managers manage their people. It asked amongst other questions, if people knew what was expected of them; if they had the right materials and equipment for their job; if they had opportunities every day to do what they were good at; if they had received recognition or praise in the previous seven days and if someone seemed to care about them and gave them encouragement. These were amongst the important factors that were responsible for the sales and profit figures that had come out of the research.

Alongside the management development programme, they had introduced a pilot approach to team development and individual coaching for various business teams that they called 'Reach for the Stars'. With his keen interest in sport, Douglas had for some time wondered why top sports teams engaged a team of professionals to assist them reach peak performance, whereas in most organisations, business teams might get a token 'Away Day' once a year. The professionals involved with sports teams included, obviously, a coach as well as usually a fitness expert, a nutritionist, a psychologist, a doctor, a physiotherapist and masseur. What Douglas had found increasingly peculiar was that business teams were expected to achieve peak performance day in day out, week after week, year after year, without often any real support. 'Silver Waters' had engaged an outside business to provide this service to those teams who chose to become involved. The support they were offered included personal coaching, health, fitness and nutritional advice and assistance, including stress management, and building strong internal team dynamics.

'Reach for the Stars' had been running for eighteen months and those teams involved had responded well with rising performance levels and much lower absence rates.

Douglas reflected with great pride on the fact that the various innovations that he and his management team colleagues had introduced had reduced people turnover to around 5% – just enough, they had thought, to keep 'new blood' flowing through the business. And, they had saved a fortune on recruitment costs, partly through their succession planning linked to their individual development opportunities, and through a scheme whereby if a current colleague recommended a friend or acquaintance for a post, and they stayed in post for 12 months, the recommender received a bonus representing 5% of the first year's salary of their new colleague. Both these approaches had dramatically reduced the fees paid to recruitment consultants and headhunters.

Douglas was experiencing a mixture of real satisfaction of what 'Silver Waters' had achieved and a sense of sadness that it had come to an end. His way of overcoming this was to come back into the present and enjoy the moment before beginning to look forward to what lay ahead. As he stretched his arms out in front, Tara started to respond slowly standing up and stretching out at the same time, tail wagging in anticipation of an imminent move.

"Not just yet old thing." he patted Tara on the head that seemed to convey the right message to her as she settled back down at Douglas's feet releasing an audible sigh as she settled her head on her paws once again.

"A few more things to review then we'll be off for some food." Tara's ears pricked up at the mention of that word.

'Personal Development Budgets' was next on Douglas's report. Another innovation of which he was proud and which had reaped benefits in many different ways. The PDB as it had become known, was earned annually by each colleague after they had been employed for one year. At this point they were awarded a sum of £1,000 to spend on their own personal development in whichever way they wanted. All they had to do was provide receipt or some other form of proof that they had used the money for their own development, and the development did not require to be necessarily related to their work activities. Some people, for example, had used it to start learning a musical instrument, or take singing lessons. Some had used it to learn foreign languages and others on yoga and Tai Chi classes. The range of activities was fascinating; a fact that had excited Douglas about how creative and in many cases, enterprising people could be given the opportunity.

Not everyone took the opportunity to spend their PBP which started anew in each calendar year and increased by £100 over a five-year period to a maximum of £1500.

This was a life enhancing opportunity which Douglas believed benefited both the individuals, the colleagues who worked with them, and the business itself.

'The Big Idea' was next in line for scrutiny and reflection. Douglas knew that the way to grow the business and engage his colleagues in 'Our Business' there had to be a mechanism or mechanisms for people to put forward ideas for developing or improving their part, or another part of the business. It is often the case that someone operating outside a team can provide insights to that team that they themselves can't see. The big problem with that, Douglas had realised at 'Guardian Angel,' is that people become very protective of their patch and defend against any feedback or ideas from outside. They engaged in what an old friend of Douglas's liked to call 'preciosity.' Douglas had never been sure if such a word existed, liking it so much though, he had not ventured to check it in the dictionary. I digress, Douglas thought to himself as he remembered these lengthy and highly stimulating intellectual discussions with his old friend Andrew.

He had realised, together with his colleagues, that if they were to tap into the creative capacity of their workforce, they had to find a way of allowing new ideas to flow freely throughout the organisation.

They had struck on the idea of using the concept of uploading which was used by the geeks – as Thomas Freiedman had called them in his book 'The World is Flat.'

The way into this process was through their Intranet, which Douglas had insisted was of outstanding quality and updated frequently. Within their Intranet they created a 'Big Idea' site to which everyone could gain access. It had been emphasised that the idea didn't necessarily have to be 'big' in business terms; the term was used in recognition that all ideas were 'big', as in potentially useful. And anyway, it had a good ring about it he had thought. When logging onto the site, people were met with graphics and a voice that greeted them with 'What's the Big Idea Today?' The site was easy to access and use.

'Stealing' the idea from the 'geeks,' they created a similar process to that they used in developing a source code. When someone had an idea that they believed would be beneficial to the business, they posted their idea on the site. Together with the idea, they had to provide what they considered the benefits would be, and where possible, some idea of any costs involved in implementing it, as well as any people deployment issues. The individual or group had to put their name on the idea together with their password. This had a two-fold benefit. It meant that people could be rewarded for ideas that were implemented, and it stopped any ideas that could be posted in bad taste or simply as a joke.

The idea stays live for a period of two weeks, during which time anyone else can add to, or develop the original idea, also adding their name to the site. At the end of a two week period the idea is removed from the site by a member of 'Our Learning' team, processed into a proposition and forwarded to the appropriate individual or team to asses its feasibility. A response has then to be posted on the 'Big Idea' site within thirty days. All people involved in creating the idea are rewarded – if it is implemented – commensurate with the impact on the business and on their contribution to the process.

'Not without its difficulties', Douglas had written in his notes. Truly an understatement he laughed to himself. The process had taken some time to sort itself out with challenges around response times, level of impact on the business and individual contributions. Set against the background of their 'Our Business' culture, however, it had become a vital tool in taking the business forward.

People who weren't confident of using the Intranet could get personal assistance from the 'Our Learning' team, who took them through the process of posting or adding to an idea and in the process helped to increase the individual's competence on using the package.

Which brought Douglas very appropriately to the 'Our Learning' centre and team. This had been Pete Fisher's team's brainchild as an extension, or combination, of what would be known in most businesses as the training department and resource centre. In keeping with the 'Our Business' culture, the 'Centre' offered a wide range of self learning materials as well as support, where required, from in-house coaches. The 'Centre' was open from 8.00am until 8.00pm and accessible for all people working in 'Silver Waters.'

In association with 'Our Learning Centre' was 'The Energy Centre.' An idea that came directly from Douglas himself and of which he was very proud. The Centre was open daily, and although managed by a 'Silver Waters' employee, enlisted the expertise of outside coaches and teachers. The centre offered classes and sessions in meditation, which were regularly booked out, Tai Chi, Chi Gung, Yoga, Taoist breathing and nutritional advice. In addition, annual health checks were offered to all colleagues after their first twelve months of employment. The idea of offering these elements wasn't exclusive to 'Silver Waters' Douglas knew well. Again it was the combination of opportunities and the cultural context in which they were offered, which really made the difference. He had heard previously, he recalled, of a major travel company based in London who offered lunchtime meditation sessions that had a waiting list of people wanting to participate. There were also other businesses he had come across who were bringing spiritual principles and practices into the workplace.

Douglas had been amazed and of course, delighted by what they had achieved over a five-year period. He sometimes found it hard to believe that he had been the catalyst for the innovations within the business and ultimately for the results it was consistently producing. Although received with considerable scepticism and some cynicism to begin with, the results in all areas of what many businesses call the Balanced Scorecard spoke for themselves. Profit, Quality Standards, Customer Satisfaction, and Colleague Satisfaction had risen significantly over his term as CEO. Co-incidence? Douglas had hoped not!

One large piece of the jigsaw which had been an essential element for their culture of 'Collective Responsibility' was their Corporate Social Responsibility Programme. Over the years since they had introduced this into the business, it had become a much higher profile element within British businesses. He had noted that the then Government

Minister of State for Industry, Margaret Hodge, now had responsibility for CSR and had released a statement declaring her pleasure at this element of her responsibilities. Douglas had included it in his report as he had been rather saddened by the fact that the outcomes from implementing CSR that she had highlighted were purely economic with no reference to the social, community and spiritual benefits. He read through it again…

"I look forward to working with UK business to ensure that environmental protection and community cohesion are seen as an integral part of delivering sustainable economic growth and business prosperity."

Of course he wanted these for 'Silver Waters,' but he also wanted to genuinely make a difference for his business environment, for the community in which they operated and ultimately for the planet. He had agreed wholeheartedly with a spokesperson from the CIPD who had indicated that unless a business has embedded its values and cultural change across its operation, introducing CSR could backfire. Led initially by his 'People Team,' they had created a cross functional team to ensure true ownership of the CSR philosophy throughout the business. They had addressed a wide range of elements within their CSR Programme that Douglas had listed in his report…

- Ethical business practices
- Collective Responsibility – an obvious extension from their Cultural Development
- Biodiversity
- Energy Efficiency
- Carbon
- Waste Management including Recycling
- Community Projects

- Participation in Community Service
  Volunteers (CSV) projects
- Human Rights

As well as saving considerably on energy costs, Douglas believed that the CSR Programme had both tangible and hidden benefits. On the tangible front a report by Michael Taylor in the Industrial Education Magazine in 2003, had indicated that the top 50 companies dedicated to CSR practice 'tracked through the FTSE 4 Good UK 50 outperformed the FTSE 100 by 15% over the previous 5 years.' Results that Douglas reckoned had been mirrored within 'Silver Waters.'

On the hidden and intangible fronts, he believed they had derived and were still deriving many benefits from their commitment to CSR. Increased loyalty; a real concern for, and attachment to the community; an increased feel-good factor that reduced absences, illness and people turnover. There was also evidence to show that people did business with them because they were an ethical and environmentally friendly business. A fact that had been established in customer surveys. And finally, he though,… Douglas was coming to the end of his notes with a renewed sense of satisfaction at what he and his people had achieved.

'Events and Other Activities' was the final section before his summary and any appendices which he might add.

'Partnerships' was first in his list. A long-term commitment had been made to identify and partner with forward thinking and creative institutions such as the 'Praxis Centre' at Cranfield University. This was the part of the Management College that used non-traditional methods of management development. They had used their services successfully for a number of years.

They had also aimed to establish a Partnership Relationship with their suppliers and had become a member of the Global Business Partnership to ensure that they gained maximum benefit from these relationships.

And so to 'Events' the last item in this section. They had established three main events as part of their annual programme. The first was a bi-monthly in-house presentation from a visiting 'guru', as Douglas liked to call them. These had included successful business people, sports people, musicians, comedians, and alternative healers. They had been an outstanding success – open to all and always over subscribed. They started at 4 o'clock on the last Thursday of each month in question and were followed by drinks, light food and socialising. The sessions were also videotaped and made available in 'Our Learning' Centre.

Two 'Our Customers' Events were held each year always using a great venue, with top line speakers, interesting activities and entertainment. They had consistently aimed to surprise people with some aspect of the event, whether it be the venue itself or the entertainment and activities. Very few customers had ever turned down the invitation to attend.

The same was true of their 'Our Suppliers' Annual event. A fantastically popular event for 'Silver Waters,' had led to outstanding service from their key suppliers and in some cases had opened the door to cost reductions.

Douglas closed his eyes and took a deep breath. He had noticed over the years, in common with probably everyone else who reflected on it, that as he got older, each year seemed to be over almost before it had started. One year merging into the next so that his five years at 'Silver Waters' had been and gone in a blur of activity, challenges, highs and lows, successes, and thankfully few failures. He still felt young and vigorous on the inside, and, he had been told he looked ten years younger on the outside. A number of his friends had urged him to stay on at 'Silver Waters' or take on a new business challenge. And he knew that if he wanted to pursue this route then there would be many opportunities available to do so. He had become a much sought after speaker at Conferences and dinners, but he didn't see himself taking this role on as a full time occupation. He had been quite selective in choosing those events at which he would speak. And, he intended to continue to be so. He had, of course, considered contributing to charities and other voluntary organisations on a no fee basis and had already spoken to one or two in which he was interested.

And of course no reflection on these past years could be complete without his thoughts on Lise's contribution. In fact, he thought, almost nothing of what he had achieved would have been possible without her! She had been his catalyst, his guardian angel (he smiled to himself at that thought), his coach and confidante during the most significant period of his business life. Where she came from he still had little clue. Where she is now, he wasn't sure. He did, though, still feel her presence particularly when he had a difficult decision to make. As if she was still there prodding him and guiding him at the same time. Any thoughts of Lise always brought a smile to his face and a sense of optimism and confidence.

The sound of the river, increasing in volume in

proportion to the decrease in any traffic noise, and Tara nuzzling his hands had brought him back from his thoughts and into the present.

"Time to head back?" Tara was already on her way as he stood up and stretched out in preparation for his stroll back as the sun set and the moon rose on a beautiful late summers evening.

"Got yourself sorted out then?" Pat was sitting in their kitchen with the Champagne waiting on ice and two glasses sitting in preparation for a little celebration of his years at 'Silver Waters.'

"I just picked up the paper ten minutes ago after doing some prep for supper. Have you seen the business pages today?"

Douglas shook his head. "Haven't had time yet, been too busy tying up loose ends ready for my final departure."

"Let me read it to you… 'Guardian Angel, the one-time successful financial services business, run by Douglas Murray, the departing CEO at 'Silver Waters' has now been completely absorbed into Universal Bank, the name disappearing for ever from our corporate scene.'"

Pat paused, looking to Douglas for his response.

He simply smiled, uncorking the Champagne and filling the glasses to toast the demise of his 'first (business) love', and the success of his second.

References and Additional Suggested Reading

The Living Company	Arie de Gues 1999
The Eagles' Quest	Fred Alan Wolf 1992
Guardian Angel	Charlie Jackson 2003
The Art of Achievement	Tom Morris 2002
The Speed of Trust	Stephen MR Covey 2006
The Black Swan	Nassim Nicholas Taleb 2007
The Springboard	Stephen Denning 2001
Sophie's World	Justein Garden 1995
Open Minds	Andy Law 2001
Communication Magic	L Michael Hall 2001
Introducing NLP	Joseph O'Connor and John Seymour 2003
The World is Flat	Thomas L Friedman 2005
Keepers of the Ancient Knowledge	Joan Parisi Wilcox 1999
The Celestine Prophecy	James Redfield 1994
Secrets of the Talking Jaguar	Martin Prechtel 2002
First, Break all the Rules	Martin Buckingham and Curt Coffman
Good to Great	Jim Collins 2005
The Four Agreements	Dan Miguel Ruiz 1997
CIPD Website	www.cipd.co.uk
Way of the Peaceful Warrior	Dan Millman 1984
Gut Instinct	Pierre Pallardy 2002